a p[...]

FOR Sofia

Laura Holt-Haslam

River Pony Press

2019

Laura Holt-Haslam

To Alanna and her miniature horse, Max.

Chapter 1

Sofia removed her gloves and blew into her raw hands. Her palomino Quarter Horse snorted, steam rising from his nostrils. Ice clung to his forelock and eyelashes.

Gramma Lisa had given Sundance to Sofia for her tenth birthday last summer, and Sofia had ridden her horse nearly every day since – in rain, sweltering heat, through swarms of biting flies – but a foot and a half of ice-encrusted snow proved too big an obstacle to overcome. At least the horses had been able to stretch their legs outside for an hour this morning before the freezing rain penetrated their thick winter coats.

Sofia eased Sundance's halter over his head. The leather crown strap flopped behind his ears as she struggled to fasten the buckle. "Sorry buddy. I can't feel my fingers."

Her grandmother's bay Morgan, Delilah, shivered by the gate.

"Oh, dear. We shouldn't have turned them out." Gramma Lisa pushed her New York Giants pom-pom hat over her frizzy gray hair.

Sofia stomped her numb feet. "Can we make some hot bran mash for the horses? It would warm them up."

"As long as we can take a hot cocoa break. We need some warming up, too."

Sofia and Sundance followed Gramma Lisa and Delilah over the crunchy snow, avoiding a patch of ice forming beside the barn door. She led him into his stall, removed his halter, and rubbed his golden neck.

"Could you be a dear and give the beasties some hay?" Gramma Lisa emerged from Delilah's stall with the mare's halter in one hand and bucket in the other. "I really need to invest in some heated water buckets."

Sofia ran a hand through her dark hair, regretting leaving her hat in the mudroom. Her tight curls had frozen into stiff ringlets. If she squeezed them, would they shatter like icicles?

Gramma Lisa banged Delilah's frozen water bucket against the barn sink, grumbling under her breath. "I'm sick of this weather. Freezing rain on top of all this snow? I'm about ready to pack up and move to Florida."

"Then we could go to Disney World." Sofia tossed an armful of hay into Delilah's stall. The Morgan snatched a mouthful mid-air.

"We'll book a flight as soon as I win the lottery."

"Maybe we can ride the horses there, instead," Sofia teased.

Gramma Lisa laughed. "High Hopes Stables has a heated indoor ring. Can you believe that? People can ride their horses in a blizzard if they want."

Sofia tossed the remainder of the bale of hay into Sundance's stall. "Maybe we can bring Sundance and Delilah in the trailer?"

"I like the way you think, Sofia," Gramma Lisa said. "I'll give them a call and see if we can schedule some riding time for this afternoon."

A few hours later, they loaded the two horses for the short drive to High Hopes Stables.

The gloomy indoor ring lacked windows and was smaller than Gramma Lisa's outdoor riding area, but the footing was soft and they were protected from the biting wind. After tacking Sundance, Sofia shed her heavy winter jacket and mounted her horse.

As she trotted her gelding in a figure-eight pattern around the arena, Gramma Lisa slowed Delilah and halted. A lanky man with a scraggly beard man led an Appaloosa into the ring. Tiny white spots dusted the horse's dark chestnut coat.

The man stopped in front of Gramma Lisa and tipped his cowboy hat. "Good morning. I'm Mike. This is Geronimo. Are you new boarders?"

"I wish we were, but no, we've just paid for the privilege to escape our winter wonderland for a few hours." Gramma Lisa dismounted and extended her hand to Mike. "I'm Lisa, and that's my granddaughter, Sofia."

Mike stroked his beard and grinned at Sofia. "What a pretty girl you are, darlin."

Sofia shivered and turned Sundance away.

Mike and Gramma Lisa chatted while they meandered around the ring on their horses. Sofia cantered past, pretending not to notice as Gramma Lisa's rumbling laughter reverberated through the enclosed space. She wished her grandmother would tone it down a bit. Why was she encouraging this creepy stranger?

After twenty minutes of trotting and cantering, Sofia leaned forward in the saddle to feel Sundance's thick winter coat. His chest felt warm and damp. Though she'd brought a blanket for him, she didn't want Sundance to get chilled on the trailer ride home. She dismounted and led the palomino in slow circles around the ring.

Sundance flattened his ears as Mike and Geronimo approached him from behind.

"You've got a fine horse there," Mike said as they passed.

"Thanks." Sofia wound her fingers through Sundance's mane.

"Your grandmother must be an excellent teacher. You've got a good seat." He winked.

Sofia felt her face grow hot. Gramma Lisa had often complimented her on her good seat, but the way Mike said it made her skin prickle.

Where was Gramma Lisa? Her heart beat faster as she scanned the arena.

"I know lots of girls 'round here ride English like you, but that horse of yours is a natural Western horse. He'd take you places. You should let me show you how to ride Western." Mike dismounted. "Wanna give it a try? I can help you get on Geronimo."

Sofia spotted Gramma Lisa at the opposite end of the ring talking with a young woman who was holding a stocky, chestnut draft horse. "Not right now."

"Well, you can think about it, honey," Mike said as Sofia walked away.

***

Sofia sat cross-legged on Gramma Lisa's couch, eyes closing. Her head nodded. The pencil in her right hand slipped from her grasp and rolled across the math worksheet in her lap.

Slam.

She jerked awake. It must have been a car door. Mike's? But no, he'd left a half hour ago, after driving Gramma Lisa home from their dinner out.

Sofia pushed her homework aside and rose from the couch. She yawned and stretched before walking to the open window at the other end of the living room. The setting sun cast long shadows through the budding maple trees lining the driveway. A cool breeze caressed Sofia's face.

She didn't recognize the vehicle. A sheet of cardboard was duct-taped over the rear passenger-side door, and white paint had chipped away from the dented back bumper, sprouting patches of rust.

Bang. Bang. Bang!

Sofia hurried to the door.

"Mom? What are you doing here?" It was the first time Sofia had seen her mother since Christmas.

Mom stormed into the house, her blonde hair in tangles and her face blazing. "Where is your grandmother?"

Gramma Lisa ran from the kitchen, wiping flour onto her jeans. "What on earth?"

Mom's mouth contorted. "I should be asking you that question." She turned to Sofia. "You need to pack up your things and get in the car."

"Why?" Sofia glared at Mom. *She probably broke up with her boyfriend. Now she wants to be my mother again.*

"Because your grandmother never learns." Mom threw a furious look at Gramma Lisa. "After all these years she's still picking the wrong sorts of friends."

"What are you talking about, Mandi?" Gramma Lisa reached for Sofia's shoulder, but Mom slapped it away.

"I hear you're dating your new riding buddy," Mom said. "He sounds like a winner."

Gramma Lisa took a step toward Mom, fists balled. "And I should take dating advice from you?"

Sofia fled up the stairs and slammed her bedroom door. Mom and Gramma Lisa's angry voices shook the walls. Sofia heard a heavy thud, followed by the sound of breaking glass. Shaking, she threw herself onto her bed and pulled the covers over her face.

Would Mom force her to move again? Sofia had lost count of how many places she'd lived since her father left. Six? Seven? She'd lived with Gramma Lisa for nearly a year, most of it without Mom.

Footsteps echoed through the hall. Sofia rolled into a ball and whimpered.

The door creaked open.

"Honey Bear?"

Sofia heard Mom enter her bedroom, but she didn't move.

Mom peeled the blankets from her trembling body. "We need to get your things together. You can't stay at Gramma Lisa's anymore."

"Why not?"

Mom rubbed Sofia's back. "It's for your own good. Trust me."

"Where are you taking me?"

"Auntie Helen has agreed to let us stay with her for a few weeks, until we can find another place."

Sofia buried herself under the blankets and sobbed. Auntie Helen's apartment smelled like dirty socks.

Mom stroked the blanket covering Sofia's head. "Oh, Honey Bear. Don't cry. There's so much to do around Boston. Maybe we can go to the aquarium together and watch the penguins. You'll like that."

"And after that we can come home to Gramma Lisa's?"

Mom hesitated. "When I was your age, I loved spending summers in Maine with my Grampy. There's the ocean and lakes and mountains and fresh air. Maybe he'll let us spend the summer with him at his house."

Sofia's throat tightened. "What about Sundance?"

"You know we can't bring him. Where would we keep him?"

Sofia tore off her blankets and pushed herself into a sitting position. "He's my horse, Mom. I can't leave him behind."

Mom stood. "Your grandmother will take care of him. Now get out of that bed and start packing."

"No!" Sofia pounded her fist into the mattress. "I'm not leaving!"

An hour later, Mom's car tore out of Gramma Lisa's driveway. Sofia clutched her pillow, weeping in the back seat.

Chapter 2

Sofia giggled as velvety lips brushed her outstretched hand. A tiny pinto horse bit into the apple with a loud crunch. He chewed, closed his eyes, and began to suck on his tongue. Frothy drool dribbled down his chin.

She'd discovered the barn and two miniature horses while exploring Grampy's neighborhood earlier that morning. Sofia returned to the horses' paddock bearing gifts – three mushy apples and two wilting carrots rescued from the back of Grampy's refrigerator. She barely knew her great-grandfather, but she'd be stuck living with him for the rest of the summer. At least his house didn't smell like dirty socks.

A chestnut mare approached the fence. Her narrow blaze looked like white paint that had splattered onto her forehead and dribbled in an uneven line down the left side of her face. The little horse's nose peeked through the fence and nuzzled Sofia's thigh.

The pinto flattened his ears and pushed his companion away, clearly the boss.

"Don't be such a sourpuss. You won't get any friends that way," Sofia teased.

In response, the horse raised his upper lip and smacked loudly. *What a goofy little guy.* Sofia laughed and fed him another apple.

"You're adorable." She reached through the wooden fence boards and stroked the pinto's long black and white forelock. How unusual for a horse to have one brown ear and one white ear. But grabbing her attention were the pinto's eyes—both blue. She had never seen a blue-eyed horse before.

Sofia's own eyes were a rich, coffee brown, like her Dominican father's. He'd loved to dance, his hand on Mom's hip, drawing her close, touching her freckled face, laughing. He called it Bachata. Sofia guarded these precious fragments of memory, yet they continued to slip away, disappearing from her life as her father had so many years ago.

The chestnut mare lifted her head, pricked her ears forward and stared intently into the distance. A moment later, Sofia heard it, too. Tires crunching over gravel. She froze, unsure of how to respond before backing away from the fence. She dashed for her bike and mounted it just as a red pickup truck rounded the corner and came into view.

The vehicle stopped abruptly and the driver rolled down her window. "What are you doing here? This is private property."

Sofia's bike wobbled as she struggled to find her balance while clutching the remaining apple and carrots in her left hand. The horses' treats tumbled to the ground.

The woman in the red truck narrowed her eyes. "Are you feeding my horses?"

Blinking back tears, Sofia raced down the driveway, not daring to look back.

The miniature pinto and tiny chestnut mare were the first horses Sofia had touched since leaving Gramma Lisa's house nearly two months ago. She'd hoped she might be allowed to help the neighbor care for them. But she'd blown it. She'd trespassed on private property and fed the horses without asking first, and now the lady in the red pickup truck must hate her.

Does Sundance remember me?

Sofia leapt up the porch steps two at a time and rushed through the door of her great-grandfather's house.

Grampy looked up from his newspaper and frowned. "What are you in such a rush about?"

She quickly wiped her sleeve across her eyes. Wetness still clung to her long, black eyelashes. She hoped he didn't notice. Old people don't always see that well.

Sofia took a slow breath and tried to calm her voice. "I'm sorry, Grampy."

"You seem all worked up."

"No. I'm fine."

"Humph." Grampy's bushy, white mustache fluttered as he exhaled.

Sofia shoved her hands into her pockets to steady them. "May I go to the guest room?"

Grampy nodded. "I keep telling you it's your room now. Make yourself at home."

Sofia forced herself to walk calmly to *her* room, eased the door shut, and flopped onto the bed. She allowed the tears to flow freely, but muffled her sobs with her pillow.

She wondered how long Mom would stay angry with Gramma Lisa. Every time Sofia mentioned it, Mom scowled and told her to stop asking. When Sofia had tried to call Gramma Lisa from Auntie Helen's phone, Mom flipped out. Did Grampy know that Mom had forbidden her to speak with her grandmother? Maybe she could wait until Grampy was asleep and then use his phone.

What Sofia needed was a cell phone. Her mom couldn't go two minutes without texting her newest boyfriend or scrolling through her social media feeds, but refused to even consider Sofia's request for one.

"It's not healthy for kids your age to have phones. You need to be outside getting fresh air, not staring at a tiny screen all day," Mom had told her.

There wasn't much of a danger of excessive screen time in this house. Grampy didn't even own a computer. All he had was an old television that blasted talk shows, sports, and news all day and night, even when he wasn't home. Maybe when a person got to be eighty years old they didn't worry about ruining their hearing anymore. Or maybe Grampy had already ruined his hearing from listening to music turned up way too loud, like Gramma Lisa always warned would happen to Sofia.

A quiet knock on the door interrupted her thoughts.

"I made some mac 'n cheese if you're up for it," Grampy said.

She opened the door and followed her great-grandfather to the kitchen table.

Grampy lifted a pile of magazines and junk mail from Sofia's seat and placed it on the wobbly metal stand beside his ancient television set. "Would you like some milk?"

Sofia nodded. "Thanks."

Grampy scowled at his TV while they ate. The Red Sox were losing to the Yankees by two runs.

Sofia arranged her peas to form a circle around the rim of her plate before picking at the remnants of her macaroni.

"I'm sure it's hard for you, missing your mother and all."

Sofia didn't look up. "I guess so."

She wasn't entirely sure she did miss Mom. Not yet, anyway. It had only been a week since Mom left for England. She hated to admit that, even to herself. What kind of daughter wouldn't miss her own mother?

Grampy's fork clinked against his plate. He sipped his Diet Coke. The Yankees pitcher struck the Red Sox batter out, ending the inning.

"Lisa tells me you're quite the horseman," Grampy said.

Horsewoman. "I guess so."

When had Grampy spoken with Gramma Lisa? It was hardly fair that he could talk with her when Sofia couldn't, even if Gramma Lisa was his former daughter-in-law. Sofia mashed her peas into the remaining macaroni and cheese and put down her fork.

"My neighbor, Stephanie, has horses. The miniature kind," Grampy said.

Heat rose in Sofia's cheeks. She hoped Grampy wouldn't notice.

"I was thinking that maybe tomorrow morning I could introduce you."

Sofia swallowed, imagining various ways Stephanie might react when Grampy introduced her. *You're the trespasser who fed my horses! How dare you come here again? I'm calling the police and having you arrested.*

Her stomach churned, and she pushed her plate away.

Chapter 3

When Sofia drifted into a fitful sleep she dreamed of trotting Sundance in a large, open field. Bright sunshine warmed her face. Knee-high grass swished under her horse's feet.

Honk. Honk. Honnnk!

Startled, Sofia looked over her shoulder to see a red pickup truck hurtling towards them. It swerved past, frightening Sundance, who whirled and almost unseated Sofia. She regained her balance and urged Sundance into a gallop, desperate to escape the vehicle. A stone boundary wall loomed before them, separating the field from thick woods. Sundance leaped over the wall, but Sofia lost her stirrups and tumbled headfirst into the rocks.

She awoke with a gasp. Her blankets lay tangled on the floor.

During breakfast, Sofia picked at her Frosted Flakes. She felt like a large worm had attached itself to her stomach lining and sucked her insides raw.

Grampy sipped his coffee, appearing more interested in his newspaper than the blaring television. A half-hour passed with no mention of visiting his angry neighbor. Sometimes old people forgot what they promised to do. Maybe Grampy was getting dementia. That would be a bad thing, of course, but maybe it could work in Sofia's favor this one time.

"Humph." Grampy pushed aside the sports section and stood. "Well, it's about time we get going and meet Stephanie."

Sofia swallowed to keep from throwing up.

Grampy reached for a blue windbreaker draped carelessly on the back of a kitchen chair. "It's a nice morning. Stephanie only lives about a quarter mile down the road. Let's walk."

As they walked down the quiet road, surrounded by woods on one side and a hay field on the other, Grampy whistled. The tune sounded slightly familiar. Was it a Christmas carol? In June? They crossed the road and turned down a winding, gravel driveway.

Sofia shivered despite the warmth of the morning. What would this woman say to Grampy when she recognized Sofia?

They passed a thicket of evergreen trees and a small, ranch-style house came into view on Sofia's right. A white, three-railed fence enclosed a horse paddock to her left. The paddock connected to a small barn with a metal roof, and behind that, an overgrown pasture. Sofia spotted the two miniature horses. The chestnut mare looked up from her hay.

A tall woman emerged from the barn, pushing a wheelbarrow half-filled with wood shavings and horse manure. Her long, blonde hair was streaked with purple highlights. Sunlight glinted off the silver stud in her nose. She wore cut-off shorts and brightly patterned rubber boots.

She was not the angry woman from yesterday, but Sofia ducked behind Grampy just to be safe.

"Hi, Mr. Richardson. Long time no see," the young woman said.

"Grace. How's life as a hard-working college student?"

"Never been better." Grace put down the wheelbarrow beside a picnic table and gave Grampy a hug.

"I bet your mom's happy you're home for the summer."

Grace shrugged. "As long as I muck every day and scrub the water buckets, I guess she'll put up with me for a while." She tilted her head at Sofia. "And who's this? Your granddaughter?"

"Actually, she's my great-granddaughter, Sofia Ruiz. She's staying with me for a while."

Grace smiled. "Nice to meet you."

Sofia returned her smile, but didn't let her guard down. This friendly girl wasn't the woman from the red truck, but any minute now that woman might storm out of the house to confront her.

Grampy gestured toward the barn. "Is your mother home? I thought maybe Stephanie would let Sofia visit your ponies. She's a real horse lover."

"Another horse lover in the neighborhood!" Grace raised her hand for a high-five. Sofia reluctantly tapped Grace's palm. "Mom's at work, but I'd be happy to show you around, if it's okay with your great-grandfather."

Sofia exhaled. She hadn't realized she'd been holding her breath.

"If you don't mind, I think I'll just have a seat at your picnic table." Grampy eased himself onto one end of the wooden bench and groaned.

Grace pushed the wheelbarrow to the edge of the driveway and led Sofia past Grampy to a metal gate beside the barn. "Come on in and meet the minis."

Sofia entered the paddock. Grace had barely closed and latched the gate when the little pinto gelding trotted up to Sofia and began nuzzling her pockets.

"Naughty boy, Snickers. She doesn't have anything for you." Grace turned to Sofia. "Sorry. This boy always used to mug for treats. He doesn't usually do it anymore. He's not allowed to eat stuff like that."

Sofia examined the mud on her shoes. Her heart pounded uncomfortably. What would Grace say when she found out she'd fed Snickers? Would she be told to leave and never come back? Sofia hadn't known it was against the rules. Grace seemed like a friendly, kind person, but Sofia knew people who appear nice can still hurt you. Admitting her mistake would be risky, but the truth would come out the second Grace's mother showed up.

Maybe it was better to just get it over with.

"Actually... I visited him yesterday, and I gave him some apples. I'm really sorry. Your mother got pretty upset and—"

Grace laughed. "Oh, I can imagine. She gets really overprotective of Snickers. Don't feel bad. You didn't know."

Grace bent and flung her arms around Snickers' neck. "You poor, little, starving boy. You know what the vet says. No sugar for you." She kissed him on the nose, and turned back to grin at Sofia.

"Snickers loves candy. He lives for it! He will do absolutely anything for peppermints. Seriously, all you have to do is crinkle the wrapper and he will jump through a hoop of fire if you ask him. Once, when I was really little, I snuck him a marshmallow peep from my Easter basket. All that gooey, yellow goodness... He was in heaven. So every Easter after that, I always gave him half of my peeps- you know half for me, half for him. He loves pop-tarts, too. Especially blueberry."

Sofia smiled as she imagined how Gramma Lisa might react if she fed Sundance marshmallows. "Why isn't Snickers allowed to eat candy now?"

"He got pretty fat. Well, he's still too fat, actually. But a few years ago he developed a condition called laminitis. Have you heard of it?"

Sofia shook her head.

Grace pointed to her thumb. "You know how your fingernail is attached to your finger? Imagine what it would feel like if the tissue under your fingernail swelled up. That would hurt, wouldn't it?"

Sofia nodded, wondering what fingernails had to do with a horse getting sick.

"A horse's hoof is kind of like a fingernail, only a lot thicker. When a horse gets laminitis, the tissues that connect a horse's hoof to the coffin bone in his foot begin to swell. It's incredibly painful, and can make a horse so lame he can barely walk. If it gets bad enough the horse sometimes has to be put down."

"And eating sugar causes laminitis?" Sofia fed Sundance treats almost every day when she lived with Gramma Lisa, and he never got laminitis.

"It can in certain horses, like Snickers. Our vet did some blood tests and we discovered Snickers' insulin levels were really high. That's probably why he got laminitis in the first place, and it puts him at risk for getting it again. His body can't handle extra sugar, so he has to have a special diet."

"And apples are bad, too?" Sofia always thought apples were healthy.

"Believe it or not, apples contain quite a bit of natural sugar. Mom likes to be on the safe side, so she has a no-treat rule. In fact, Snickers isn't even allowed to eat green grass."

"What does he eat, then?" Sofia couldn't imagine what it must be like for a horse not to be allowed to eat grass. This must be why the horses were kept in a dirt paddock instead of in the large pasture area behind the barn.

"Hay. It's safer than grass because it's lower in sugar. And he gets a supplement with vitamins and other stuff he needs."

The gelding pushed his nose against Sofia's leg. *I'm not giving you any more treats, Mister.*

"Cut it out, Snickers." Grace shook her finger at the pinto. "He belongs to my brother. But Kevin hardly ever sees him because he's serving in the Marines. Do you want to meet my little sweetie-pie? Her name is Kit Kat. I've had her since I was four."

Compared with Snickers' blue eyes and brown, black, and white coloring, Kit Kat's chestnut coat seemed rather ordinary, but Sofia had to admire the dainty mare's large, intelligent-looking eyes and tiny ears. She was even smaller than Snickers, and definitely trimmer. "Did you ride her when you were little?"

Grace shook her head. "She's too small for anyone to ride. I had a few pony rides on Snickers when I was really little. But Mom used to own a big horse named Toby, and we all rode him. We used to take him to shows. I won tons of blues on him."

"He sounds really awesome. You don't have him anymore?" Sofia asked.

Grace sighed. "Toby died almost two years ago, right after I left for college."

"That's sad. I'm sorry." Sofia didn't want to think about how awful it would be if something happened to Sundance.

"Mom took it really hard. He was her baby before Kevin and I were even born."

Sofia stroked Kit Kat's neck. "I miss my horse, too. He didn't die, but I haven't seen him for a while."

Grace clapped her hands. "Oh, you have your own horse! I want to know all the juicy details."

Sofia smiled. "His name is Sundance, and he's a palomino Quarter Horse."

"Toby was a Quarter Horse, too," Grace said, "Only he was a bay. With a star on his forehead."

"Sundance has a blaze. And two white stockings on his hind legs."

"I bet he's beautiful," Grace said. "Do you ride him English or Western?"

"My grandmother taught me how to ride English. But her boyfriend wants me to show Sundance in Western..." Sofia's voice trailed off.

Grampy wandered over to the paddock. "You ladies seem to be having fun."

"Sure are," Grace said. "Would it be okay if Sofia hangs out here with me for a while? I was thinking she can help me finish the chores and groom the minis."

Grampy turned to Sofia. "Would you like that?"

Sofia rubbed her palms together and nodded. "I can muck out the paddock. And clean the water buckets. I'm good at that."

Grace laughed. "So I can just stand back and watch you do the work? Sounds like a plan."

Sofia scrambled through the fence rails and grabbed the pitchfork from Grace's wheelbarrow. "I'll see you later, Grampy."

***

Sofia inhaled the scent of horse sweat and manure. Some people thought this smell was disgusting, but she couldn't imagine a more satisfying aroma. She rubbed a curry comb in circles over Snickers' body, producing a cloud of dust and loose fur. Reaching into the grooming box, Sofia pulled out a hard-bristled brush. With short, quick strokes, she flicked the dirt from the miniature horse's back and rump.

Grace pulled a tangle from Snickers' black and white tail. "You'd think no one ever grooms him, but I did yesterday. Seriously."

Sofia nodded. "I know what you mean. Sundance loves to roll in the mud right after I brush him."

"What a stinker," Grace said. "And they step in poop after you pick out their hooves."

Sofia laughed and ran her hand down Snickers' leg, gently lifting his tiny foot. He did indeed have manure wedged into his hoof, but she didn't mind. She carefully pried it out with a hoof pick.

Grooming the horses had been one of her favorite activities when she lived with Gramma Lisa. The first few times she'd tried to pick out Sundance's feet, she feared being stepped on or kicked, but she'd learned to trust him.

"Have you ever driven in a cart with a horse?" Grace asked.

Sofia shook her head.

"Do you want to try? Snickers could use some exercise." Grace poked Snickers' belly.

Sofia's stomach lurched. She didn't know how to drive a horse. What if Snickers galloped out of control and smashed up the cart? Grace's angry mother would ban Sofia from the barn for sure. "Umm...will you show me what to do?"

"Of course." Grace pointed to a large, purple bag hanging on the barn wall. "Snickers' driving harness is in there. Why don't you unzip it and I'll show you how to put it on."

Looking into the bag, Sofia's eyes widened. The bag overflowed with complicated-looking leather straps and pieces. She'd required several weeks of practice before feeling confident saddling and bridling Sundance by herself. Even then Gramma Lisa always checked her work before Sofia was allowed to mount up. How could she possibly learn how to harness a horse?

Only one piece looked somewhat familiar to Sofia. She removed the tiny bridle from the tangle of leather. The bit looked like a toy. She doubted whether this bridle could even fit around Sundance's nose.

Sofia pointed to the shiny leather squares attached to the sides of the bridle. "What are those for?"

"They're called blinders." Grace touched the corners of her blue eyes. "Horses' eyes are different from peoples' eyes. We see what's in front of us, but horses can see almost all the way around to their tails without even turning their heads. The blinders make it so they can't see the cart behind them and get afraid or distracted by it."

"Blinders," Sofia repeated, trying to memorize the word.

"Or some people call them blinkers. And other people call them winkers."

"That's confusing." It was bad enough that there were about a million different straps. What if each part had multiple names? Sofia would never learn them all.

"Well, you'd better pay attention, because there's going to be a quiz," Grace said.

Sofia let out a quick breath. "Really?"

Grace laughed. "I'm just kidding. But when I was your age, I was in a horse club called the Mini Whinnies. Mom was our leader, and she wouldn't let us ride in the cart until we had memorized all the parts of the harness, what they were used for, and how to put them on."

"You were in a horse club?" As much as the idea of having to memorize all the parts of the harness intimidated her, she'd love to join a horse club and meet some other kids. "Is the Mini Whinnies club still around?"

"It died out when I was in high school. But it was fun while it lasted," Grace said. "We went to lots of shows with Kit Kat and Snickers and Mom's horse, Toby. And we dressed the minis in silly costumes. We even marched in a few parades."

"That's awesome! I would totally join your club."

Grace looked past Sofia, staring vaguely at a pitchfork hanging on the wall. After a long pause she said, "You know, maybe we can restart the club."

"Really?" With great effort, Sofia prevented herself from jumping up and down. She didn't want to frighten Snickers, after all.

"Why not? You're here for the summer. I'm here for the summer. Snickers and Kit Kat could use the exercise."

Snickers whinnied.

Sofia laughed. "I think he's excited, too."

Chapter 4

Sofia stood outside the barn rubbing Snickers' tiny chin. She wondered how she'd ever learn to fasten all those straps to his cart.

"One of the rules for Mini Whinnies is to wear a helmet when driving." Grace handed Sofia a green riding helmet. "Hopefully, it will fit."

Sofia had her own riding helmet— lilac-colored and embellished with blue swirls and the profile of a horse with flowing mane— but it hung on the wall of Gramma Lisa's tack room in Connecticut. She tugged at the chin strap to tighten the green helmet.

"Do you want to hold Snickers while I connect the cart to him?" asked Grace.

Sofia nodded. At least she knew how to do that job.

Grace positioned the two-wheeled cart behind the pinto's rump and eased the metal shafts forward, placing them into loops at Snickers' sides. "These are called the tugs. Once I position the shafts, I tighten this piece next to his girth. That holds the tugs in place, so they don't slip up or down too much."

That part didn't look too complicated.

Grace grabbed a long, thick strap of leather that was attached to the breast collar of Snickers' harness. "These are called the traces." She slid the slotted end of the strap through a swiveling bar on the front of the cart. "Traces prevent the cart from slipping out of the tugs when the horse moves forward."

"And next is the breeching." Grace wrapped a strap around the metal shaft of the cart, through a loop, and around the shaft again before buckling it into place. "This stops the cart from slipping forward. We wouldn't want it to hit Snickers in the rear end."

Sofia frowned in concentration.

"I know it's a lot to learn, but you'll figure it out, I promise. It just takes practice."

Grace buckled her helmet. Its color nearly matched the purple streak in her hair. "The driver always gets in first." She took the reins and climbed into the cart.

Snickers stepped forward and Sofia grabbed his bridle to steady him.

"Stand," Grace commanded. She patted the seat. "I'm ready when you are."

Sofia inhaled, let go of Snickers' head, and approached the side of the cart. As she scrambled in, the gelding shifted in his harness.

"He hasn't been driven for a while," Grace said. "But he's about to get a work-out. Ready?"

"I think so," Sofia said.

"Snickers, trot!"

The horse lurched forward.

Sofia clutched the side of the cart, afraid of tumbling out. The cart bounced slightly to the two-beat rhythm of Snickers' trotting. She exhaled and relaxed her grip.

Snickers' pace slowed. Grace made a kissing sound and his speed increased. They raced down the driveway before Grace eased back the reins. "Slow... Walk."

The pinto responded almost instantly.

"Do you want to try holding the reins?" Grace asked.

"Me?"

"I don't..." Grace swung her head from side to side, "... see anyone else in the cart."

"But what if I do something wrong?"

"I'm right here. I'll take over if anything bad happens."

Grace handed the reins to Sofia. "It's just like when you ride, except that you're a lot further away. Now ask him to walk on."

"Um... Walk on, Snickers." To her astonishment, Snickers listened. She didn't even have to slap the reins on his back like they do in the movies.

"Now why don't you turn him in a big circle around that tree." Grace pointed to a huge maple.

"What if I crash into it?"

"Make sure you don't start your turn until the cart passes the tree. You'll be fine."

I can do this. Sofia pulled on the left rein and Snickers began to turn just a little. She tugged harder and he turned more sharply, his right front leg crossing in front of his left.

"Look at that. Great job! And guess who's coming down the driveway?"

With a jolt, Sofia recognized the red truck. She wanted to hide but there was no place to go.

Stephanie turned off the ignition, opened the door, and stepped out. "Grace, who's your new friend?"

"This is Sofia. She's Mr. Richardson's great-granddaughter."

Stephanie squinted at Sofia. "Aren't you the kid I caught feeding the horses yesterday?"

Sofia ducked her head, waiting for Stephanie to yell at her. At least Grampy wasn't here to witness her humiliation.

Grace draped her arm around Sofia's shoulder and squeezed. "She didn't know. She just misses her horse, and wanted to get to know Kit Kat and Snickers. And look. She's doing an awesome job driving."

Grace took the reins from Sofia's shaking hands and whispered, "Go on. I promise she doesn't bite."

Heart racing, Sofia climbed out of the cart.

Like Grace, Stephanie was a tall woman, though somewhat thicker around the middle. She peered down at Sofia with icy blue eyes. "Well, young lady, since you have a bit of experience around horses, you should know better than to feed someone's horse without asking permission."

Sofia gulped. "I'm so sorry, ma'am. I will never do that again."

The corner of Stephanie's mouth twitched. "You don't need to call me ma'am. Please just call me Stephanie. Apology accepted."

Sofia's eyes widened. *Really?* She turned to look at Grace, who nodded.

Maybe Stephanie didn't hate her after all.

***

"Goodness, Sofia." Grampy added a third sandwich to Sofia's plate. "Either you think I'm a gourmet chef, or you're really hungry."

"Thanks, Grampy. You make awesome grilled cheese."

"After your Grammy passed, I got real good at making them. Just add a can of tomato soup and you've got yourself a first-class lunch."

Sofia downed a second glass of milk and reached for a package of Oreos. She smiled as she imagined what Snickers might think of the cookies. Of course, she'd never give him one now that she knew he could get sick. Maybe Kit Kat would like one. But that might not be the best idea, either. She didn't want Stephanie to get upset with her again.

The ringing phone interrupted Sofia's thoughts.

"Hello? Mandi?" Grampy wandered across the kitchen and turned down the television. "Yes, she's been very good... No, not a problem at all... She's right here."

Grampy passed the receiver to Sofia. "It's your mother."

Sofia took a deep breath. She hadn't spoken to Mom since she and Grampy dropped Mom off at the airport last week. "Hi."

"Honey Bear! How are you doing? You're being good for Grampy, right? Not giving him any trouble?"

"No, I've been good."

"It's so great to hear your voice, baby girl. I miss you bunches and bunches."

Then why did you leave me here? Oh, yeah. 'Cause of him.

"You wouldn't believe Paul's house. It's practically a castle. I can't wait for you to see it."

Sofia paced in circles as Mom described the quaint pub in Paul's village and what kind of food they served there. The cord from the telephone wrapped around and around her. She turned the other direction and unwound herself. When she pulled on it, it stretched. She let go and it bounced. Grampy's phone belonged in a museum, but at least it provided mild entertainment.

"So, Honey Bear, has Grampy taken you anywhere fun?" Mom asked.

Sofia stopped twirling. "I visited his neighbor's miniature horses this morning. And I got to brush them and I even got to drive in the cart while Snickers pulled it."

"Who is Snickers?"

"One of the miniature horses. He's a bay pinto. With two blue eyes."

"Well, that sounds fun."

"Yeah, it was. And Grace and Stephanie said I can visit the horses whenever I want. They invited me to help them feed and do the chores on Monday morning. And Grace wants to teach me how to harness and drive Snickers all by myself. We're going to start a horse club called the Mini Whinnies, and we might even go to a horse show."

"Well that's great, Sofia. It's nice that you'll get to play with the horses." Mom paused. "Don't get too attached though, honey."

Sofia suddenly regretted eating three grilled cheese sandwiches. *Don't get too attached.* That's what Mom had said about Sundance, too.

Sofia blinked back tears. "Do you want to talk with Grampy again?"

"What? Oh, sure. You have lots and lots of fun there in Maine. I'll be back before you know it. Love you, Honey Bear!"

"Love you, too, Mom," Sofia mumbled. She handed the phone to Grampy and retreated to the bathroom, locking the door behind her.

Chapter 5

Sofia had never attended a church service, at least not as far as she could recall, but she had seen enough churches on television to know they were boring. People were supposed to dress in fancy clothes and sit on wooden benches and listen to a man talk for a long time. Sometimes the man was so boring the people actually fell asleep, but you had to be careful because other times the preacher screamed at people and made them feel guilty. At least Grampy promised they'd serve ice cream afterwards.

"What am I supposed to wear?" Sofia had only one dress, and it was unbearably itchy and a size too small for her. Even if she owned a closet full of dresses, she wouldn't wear one if she could possibly help it.

Grampy blew out a long breath. "It doesn't matter. Wear whatever you want."

And so, on Sunday morning, she emerged from her room wearing a bright pink tee-shirt that proclaimed "I'd rather be mucking."

Grampy narrowed his eyes and stared at her for a moment, then asked if she wanted toast and scrambled eggs for breakfast.

An hour later, they climbed five concrete steps leading to the large, wooden double doors of the Good Shepherd Community Church. More stairs led to a large room with a high ceiling and stained glass windows. Sofia hoped Grampy would allow her to sit in the back where no one would notice her. Unfortunately, her great-grandfather insisted that his pew was the fourth one from the front on the left side. That's where he sat every Sunday morning, behind two elderly ladies, who Grampy introduced as Mrs. Sylvia Smith and her sister, Mrs. Ruth Weaver.

Mrs. Weaver grasped Sofia's hands. "It's so nice to finally meet you." The woman's dentures shifted in her mouth as she spoke, as if her teeth had a mind of their own.

Trying not to stare, Sofia muttered a barely audible "Thank you," and looked away.

Mrs. Smith fingered one of Sofia's tight, bouncy ringlets. "What beautiful hair you have, dear. I wish mine would curl like that."

Sofia shivered. Why was this stranger touching her hair?

A plump woman with blonde, shoulder-length hair stepped up to the platform at the front of the church. Could this lady be the preacher? Sofia nudged Grampy. "Is she the leader of the church?"

Grampy nodded. "That's Pastor Amy."

"Hello! And welcome. I'm so glad to see you all here on Children's Sunday."

Pastor Amy's voice thundered through the sanctuary, but Sofia thought she sounded more excited than angry. She was probably just making sure that all the old people like Grampy could hear.

"I'm so proud of all the kids for their hard work in preparing for this Children's Sunday service." Her round face radiated enthusiasm as she smiled at the children sitting in the two front pews. Sofia could only see the backs of their heads, but a few of them looked to be about her age.

A petite girl with a mass of bouncy, red curls leaned forward, taking a surprisingly long time to get to her feet. Sofia realized she needed crutches to help her to walk. They made a clacking sound each time they hit the floor. Had the girl broken both legs in an accident?

The girl made her way up two steps to the platform where Pastor Amy had been standing, and sat in a chair next to an open guitar case. Instead of wearing plaster casts, as Sofia had expected, a thick Velcro strip encircled both of her knees and wrapped around the lower part of her legs, holding plastic braces securely in place.

"Hi everyone," the girl said. "The Sunday School kids took a vote on our favorite worship songs. We picked a few for you to sing."

To Sofia's surprise, the girl leaned down, reached for the guitar, and began to play. Sofia wasn't sure what she had expected the girl to do.

Did she think that because her legs didn't work, the rest of her didn't? Clearly, that wasn't the case. She played the guitar well, maybe not perfectly, but certainly a lot better than most kids her age. And her voice! Sofia thought she could be a contestant on one of those talent search shows.

"Okay, everyone, why don't you join me for the chorus," the girl said.

Grampy and the people around Sofia stood to sing, but not from books like they did on TV. The words were projected onto a screen at the front of the church. The tune sounded unfamiliar, but Sofia tried to sing along. Her voice wavered, sounding high and scratchy, like it did when she was practicing for the fifth-grade holiday concert last December. Sadie Cohen had told her she sang like a chipmunk. Sofia closed her mouth.

The girl with the guitar led three more songs and returned to her pew.

A gangly teenage boy wandered around the room with a microphone, inviting people to share what they were thankful for. Sofia's face grow hot when Mrs. Weaver pointed to Sofia and remarked how thankful she was that Bill Richardson's great-granddaughter was here in church this morning.

Two young children raced forward to collect the offering money. A boy who looked to be about four-years-old passed the metal plate to Grampy. Sofia's eyes widened as Grampy put in three twenty-dollar bills. Grampy lived in a small, ranch-style house and he drove an old, scratched up car. He didn't seem rich.

When the little boy returned to the aisle, he tripped. The plate slid out of his hands and hit the floor with a clang, scattering its contents. A quarter rolled under Sofia's seat. She scooped it up, put it in the plate, and gathered several bills that had fallen under Mrs. Smith's pew. The boy's eyes filled with tears.

"It's okay," Sofia whispered as she gave the offering plate to the boy.

He sniffed and ran to the front of the church, nearly stumbling a second time.

Thankfully, Sofia didn't have to endure a long, boring speech. Instead, the girl with the crutches and several other kids performed a play about a mad scientist who searched for a chemical formula to make people love each other. The potion backfired, causing the lab assistant to turn into a dog. She knocked over the laboratory equipment as she chased the scientist around the church, trying to lick his face. The congregation roared with laughter, and Sofia couldn't help joining with them. At the end of the play, the girl with the crutches told the mad scientist that love comes from God, not from a chemical formula. The congregation applauded.

When the worship service finished, Pastor Amy invited everyone outside for ice cream and games. It took a while for Sofia to get down the stairs because so many people wanted to meet her. She smiled politely and shook hands with Grampy's friends while wishing she could grab a bowl of ice cream, hop into Grampy's car, and shut the door. Finally they were outside, blinking in the bright sunshine.

"Hey! I love your shirt. I'd rather be mucking, too." The red-headed girl ambled over to Sofia. "Obviously, you're into horses like I am. You're Mr. Richardson's granddaughter...no, wait. You're like his great-granddaughter, right? You're Sofia."

Sofia nodded, wondering why everyone seemed to know so much about her.

"I'm Olivia, and that's my brother, Ryan." She pointed to a slightly chubby boy with short-cropped, blond hair. Sofia recognized him as the mad scientist from the skit. "Hey, Ryan! Get your rear end over here and meet Sofia."

The boy jogged over, clutching a large bowl of chocolate ice cream, caramel sauce, and whipped cream. Some had dribbled onto his yellow polo shirt.

"Ryan, you're such a slob. I'm going to disown you."

"Not if I disown you first," Ryan said.

"No problem. Sofia can be my twin now. At least we have the same hair."

"You're a redhead. Her hair's black."

Olivia shrugged. "But we both rock the curls. And...wait for it...we both love horses."

"Okay, that's cool. But we share the same birthday, Olivia." He turned to Sofia. "Our birthday is February 26, and we're eleven. Your birthday isn't on February 26, is it?"

Sofia wanted to join in Olivia's teasing of Ryan, and pretend that she did share their birthday, but she chickened out. "July 7. I'll be turning eleven."

"See, Olivia! She can't be your twin. You're stuck with me."

Olivia whacked her brother in the knee with her crutch. "Hey, my real twin Sofia, let's get some ice cream before Ryan eats it all."

Sofia snorted, but then froze as she saw Pastor Amy stride up behind Ryan and Olivia. There had been no angry yelling from the pulpit, but Pastor Amy's stern expression caused Sofia's stomach to clench. Could church be like school? What punishments did the pastor dish out to kids when they stepped out of line?

"Olivia, cut that out," said Pastor Amy. "How many times do I have to remind you that crutches are for walking, not beating on your brother."

"Sorry, Mom."

Mom? Pastor Amy was Olivia and Ryan's mother?

"Ryan is the one you should be apologizing to," Pastor Amy said.

Pastor Amy turned to Sofia. "I'm happy to finally meet you, Sofia. Your great-grandfather has told me a lot about you."

Sofia swallowed. Grampy could go for hours hardly speaking a word to her, but it sure seemed as if he liked to talk about her with other people. Did he tell everyone at this church about her personal life?

"Mom, Sofia and I need to get our ice cream before it totally melts, okay?"

Was Pastor Amy actually rolling her eyes?

"Yes, Olivia. You and Sofia can go and get your ice cream."

***

Mrs. Smith stood in front of a plastic folding table, gripping a metal ice cream scoop. "What can I get for you girls? We've got chocolate, vanilla, and a little bit of cookies and cream."

Olivia peered into the melting remains of the cookies and cream. "What? No chocolate peanut butter cup this year? You know that's my favorite kind."

Mrs. Smith paused, ice cream scoop in mid-air. "Oh, Olivia."

"I'm the pastor's kid. I demand chocolate peanut butter cup."

Sofia wanted to disappear. She would never speak to an adult like that.

Mrs. Smith laughed, scooped a large portion of chocolate ice cream, and plopped it into Olivia's bowl. She pointed to the assortment of toppings at the other end of the table. "We have chocolate fudge, peanut butter topping, and mini peanut butter cups. Make your own, you silly girl."

"You're the best, Mrs. Smith."

"I know." Mrs. Smith turned to Sofia. "Now what can I get you, dear?"

"Umm... chocolate is good, thanks." Sofia glanced at Olivia, who had placed both crutches into her left hand and was adding generous amounts of chocolate sprinkles to her sundae.

Ryan ran to the table, nearly colliding with his sister. "Hey, Dad's going to start the games in a minute. You're going to be my partner, right?"

"What if I want Sofia to be my partner?" Olivia said.

He threw up his arms. "Come on. We're always partners."

The last thing Sofia wanted was to be caught in the center of their conflict. "You two should be partners. I can just watch."

"Are you sure?" asked Ryan.

Olivia shook her head. "No, Ryan. She's new here. You can be Michael's partner."

Ryan glared at his twin. "Fine. Be that way." He stomped off to join a circle of younger boys who were attempting to climb a huge maple tree.

Sofia jumped as a shrill note pierced the air. A balding, red-headed man blew a plastic whistle attached to an orange cord. "Let the games begin!"

Olivia nudged Sofia. "That's my dad. He's so embarrassing."

Olivia's father lifted a plastic tub filled with stuffed animals. "One of you will toss the stuffed animals to your partner, and the other one will catch them in a bucket. You'll have thirty seconds to get as many into your bucket as you can, but you'll have to catch them in the air. No picking them up after they fall on the ground."

Olivia wanted to toss the animals instead of catch them. Sofia understood why when Pastor Amy brought out Olivia's wheelchair. It would be challenging for Olivia to dart around on uneven ground while trying to catch flying stuffed animals. Being in the wheelchair would allow her to use both hands without having to balance with her crutches.

Olivia's father blew the whistle again. A purple walrus hurled towards Sofia. She raised her bucket and caught it easily. A yellow duck flew over her head, but she managed to capture a rainbow-colored octopus before it hit the ground. A unicorn smacked into her face, but then fell into the bucket. It didn't really hurt, and Sofia couldn't help laughing when she saw Olivia stick her tongue out at her. She missed three more stuffed animals in a row. After thirty seconds eight stuffed animals were in Sofia's bucket, but Ryan and Michael managed to get eleven, making them the winners.

"Ha!" Ryan wagged his finger at his twin.

"We'll beat you in the three-legged race," Olivia shouted.

How could Olivia run in a three-legged race? A half hour later, when the games ended, Sofia realized that Olivia had been kidding. There was no three-legged race. But she couldn't help but be impressed with how competitive Olivia had been racing through an obstacle course in her wheelchair.

While Pastor Amy folded up the wheelchair and lifted it into her minivan, Olivia asked, "Hey, Mom, can Sofia come over to our house this afternoon?"

"If it's okay with Mr. Richardson, it's fine with me."

You might want to ask me first.

Did Sofia want to be friends with Olivia? It wasn't like she had any other friends here, except for Grace who was pretty much a grown-up, and Snickers and Kit Kat, if you could count them as friends. She felt drawn to Olivia, yet somehow thrown off balance at the same time. Olivia was just so unpredictable, so dramatic and so *fierce*.

Five minutes later, with Olivia's father, David, at the wheel, Sofia was on her way to Olivia's house.

Chapter 6

Olivia wasn't kidding when she said she loved horses. Sofia couldn't believe that anyone could own this many model horses. Floor to ceiling shelves covered an entire wall of her bedroom. Mares, foals, stallions, famous race horses, show horses, draft horses, horses of every breed and color - each shelf must have contained twenty of them.

"Seventy-four. I've been collecting them since I was five," Olivia said. "Most of them are Breyer horses."

"This is incredible." Sofia scanned the shelves and reached for a palomino with bulging muscles. "This one kind of looks like my horse, Sundance."

"You're so lucky that you have your own horse. I wish I had one. Sundance must be gorgeous."

"He's the most beautiful horse in the world." Sofia's throat tightened.

"Elvis might disagree with you." Olivia plopped onto her bed.

"Who?"

"You're holding a model of Elvis Presley's favorite horse. He was a Quarter Horse named Rising Sun. Look, it even has a replica of Elvis' signature on the belly."

Sofia turned the plastic horse over in her hand. Sure enough, there was a signature painted in gold ink. "I think I've heard of Elvis Presley. Wasn't he a singer or something, a long time ago?"

Olivia laughed. "Uh, yeah. He was only the King of Rock and Roll... Hey, Ryan! Come here and show Sofia your Elvis impression."

Ryan trotted into Olivia's room, a silly grin plastered across his face. He stood with his legs wide apart and began to wobble his knees and wiggle his hips, singing with a low, husky voice, very unlike his own. Sofia recognized the song. Something about hound dogs crying all the time.

Ryan looked and sounded ridiculous. Sofia could barely keep a straight face.

"My brother is destined for stardom, don't you think?" Olivia waved her arms. "I can just see his name in lights."

"I'm on my way to Vegas, right after I pick up my Elvis suit," Ryan said, wiggling his hips again.

Sofia giggled. Was this what it was like to have a sibling? She often wished she had a brother or sister to share her life with. Holding onto friends had been a challenge because she moved so often. But a sibling would stay with you, ease your loneliness, understand what it was like when your father walked out on you, never to be heard from again. A brother or sister would know what it was like when your mother left you with relatives you hardly knew for months on end.

Olivia stood and transferred her right crutch to her left hand as she carefully reached for a model of a sorrel-colored draft horse. "This one is really special to me. It's custom painted to look like my favorite horse, Molly. I've been riding her since I was four."

Sofia couldn't contain her astonishment. "You ride?"

Olivia's expression hardened. "Yes, I ride. You don't think I can ride?"

"Uh, no. I didn't mean that," Sofia stammered.

"Of course you did." Olivia sat back on her bed and slammed her crutches to the floor. "Poor little handicapped girl. Obviously she can't ride. She can't even walk right."

Sofia stared at her shoes and wished she could disappear. She was just starting to believe that she and Olivia could be friends. Now she'd blown it.

"I'll have you know that I do ride. I ride every week, in fact." Olivia's voice grew shriller with each word.

Ryan reached across the bed and poked Olivia's arm. "Yeah, she rides hippos every week."

Olivia rolled her eyes and crossed her arms. Her tight lips turned up at the edges. Then she stuck out her tongue, blew a raspberry and poked Ryan back. They both cracked up.

Sofia laughed, too, glad that the tension had been broken, but confused as to what had just happened. Hippos?

"Sofia has no clue what you're talking about," said Olivia. "You should let her in on the joke."

Ryan grinned. "When we were little, Olivia started going to a riding stable for hippotherapy. Have you ever heard of that?"

Sofia shook her head.

"It's a special kind of physical therapy that they do using horses. Only for some stupid reason they call it hippotherapy." Ryan shrugged. "I was like four or something, so I was totally convinced that Olivia was getting to ride hippopotamuses every week. Horses are cool, but hippos? That's so awesome! I was really jealous, because I wanted to ride hippos, too. Mom and Dad thought it was hysterical. They've teased me about it ever since."

"But Ryan would never ride a hippo because he's a scaredy cat," Olivia said.

"Shut up, Olivia."

Olivia folded her arms. "Can you believe Ryan's never ridden a horse?"

"I have, too," Ryan protested.

"Riding a little pony at the Cumberland Fair doesn't count."

"Yes, it does." Ryan's face flushed. "Why do you have to be such a jerk?" He stomped out the door.

Maybe having a brother or sister wouldn't be so great after all.

Ryan's angry response didn't appear to bother Olivia. "Well, now that he's gone we can talk horses. Maybe we can make our own special horse club."

"I'm already in a horse club. It's called the Mini Whinnies," Sofia said.

Olivia shot Sofia a quizzical look. "No offense, but that's a weird name for a horse club. I mean, I get the Whinnies part. But…"

"It does sound dumb, I guess, except that it's a club that's about miniature horses."

Olivia's face lit up. "Those things are so adorable. We have one at my barn. Her name is Tinkerbell."

"That's a great name," Sofia said. "The two minis I know live down the street from Grampy. Snickers and Kit Kat."

"Like the candy bars?"

Sofia laughed. "Yeah, like candy bars. Only they aren't allowed to eat candy. At least Snickers isn't, because he has a problem with eating too much sugar. It makes something bad happen to his feet."

"Laminitis?"

How did Olivia know that? "Yeah."

"That's terrible," Olivia said. "There was a horse at the barn where I ride that had to be put down last year because of laminitis."

Olivia reached for the plastic model of the draft horse named Molly, which was still sitting on her pillow. She stroked its tiny face and placed it back on the shelf. "So, what do I need to do to join the Mini Whinnies?"

"Um…" Could someone like Olivia participate in the Mini Whinnies? Sofia didn't want to say the wrong thing and risk Olivia blowing up at her again. "I'll have to ask Grace."

Olivia shifted her shoulders excitedly, wiggling in place. "And you're going to see her tomorrow morning, right?"

Sofia nodded.

"It will be so fun to be in the Mini Whinnies with you, Sofia."

Sofia wondered what Grace would say when she explained that Olivia needed crutches to walk and sometimes even used a wheelchair. Wouldn't that spook the horses?

Chapter 7

Mid-morning sunlight streamed through the gaps in the curtains of Sofia's room. She turned to her side and yanked a blanket over her head. *Wait!* Today was Monday, the day she promised to help with the horses. Throwing off the covers, she launched out of the bed and staggered into the kitchen.

Grampy sat at the table wearing plaid pajamas, sipping from his coffee mug. "Good morning, Sofia."

"What time is it?" Sofia's eyes darted around the kitchen trying to find a clock.

Grampy glanced at his wrist. "Seven-twenty."

Seven-twenty? Sofia fought down a wave of panic. The horses were supposed to be fed at six-thirty. "Why didn't you wake me, Grampy?"

Grampy placed his mug on the table. "It's the summer. I thought you'd want to sleep in a bit."

"Don't you remember? I have to be at the barn to feed the horses."

"Oh, I forgot all about it." Grampy pushed back his chair and started to get to his feet.

"It's too late!" Sofia slapped her hand to her forehead. "Too late."

Grampy frowned. "Calm down, Sofia. It's going to be fine."

"No, it's not!" She ran into her room and slammed the door. Tugging off her pajamas and grabbing dirty clothes from the floor, she dressed in seconds. Not bothering with her thick tangle of hair, which could be challenging to manage even in the best of times, she dashed back to the kitchen. "I have to go, Grampy!"

"I'm not ready yet."

"Then I'm taking my bike." Heart pounding, she hurried out the door.

The morning was bright, the air warm, and choruses of birdsongs floated through the trees. Sofia pedaled her bike as fast as her legs could go, faster, faster. A squirrel jumped into the road and she swerved, barely missing it, but she managed not to slide out of control. Stephanie and Grace's house was just ahead. She turned, flew down the driveway, and skidded to a stop.

Stephanie pushed an empty wheelbarrow toward the barn. She turned as Sofia leaped off her bike. "Good morning, young lady. Or perhaps I should say good afternoon."

"I'm sorry I'm late." Sofia gasped, out of breath from her sprint to the barn. "Have they been fed yet?"

"Of course they've been fed. If I had waited for you, we'd have two very hungry horses banging their stall doors down."

Sofia grimaced as an intense cramp stabbed at her right side. "Grampy didn't wake me up."

Stephanie raised her eyebrows. "Really. So it's your Grampy's responsibility to wake you?"

Sofia didn't understand how to answer this question. She was just a kid and Grampy was a grown-up. "Umm..."

"I see you're allowed to ride your bicycle here all by yourself." Stephanie crossed her arms.

"Uh. Yeah." Sofia felt her checks grow hot.

"It seems to me that if you are old enough to ride your bike here by yourself, and mature enough to be working with horses, you should be perfectly capable of setting an alarm clock and getting yourself out of bed on time."

"I don't have an alarm clock," Sofia muttered under her breath.

"A cell phone, perhaps?"

Sofia clenched her fists. "No. I'm not allowed to have one."

"Good. You're too young for one."

Eyes filling with hot, angry tears, Sofia blurted, "You don't know anything about me!"

Stephanie narrowed her eyes. "You're right. I don't know you very well. But I do know you trespassed on my private property and fed my horses without permission. And I know that even though you told me you wanted to help with the horses, you showed up one hour late and blamed your great-grandfather instead of taking responsibility for your own actions."

Sofia felt as if she might suffocate, even as she gulped mouthfuls of air. She had to get out of there, had to escape. Her bike seemed a million steps away, but she ran for it, swung her leg over the seat and fled.

"Wait, Sofia!"

Sofia didn't look back.

***

A cloud of hungry mosquitoes buzzed around Sofia's ears as she swatted the back of her neck. Blood smeared across her palm.

She had discovered this pond a few days ago, drawn by the music of trilling frogs. It wasn't far from Grampy's house, only a few minutes on her bike. Blue swamp iris bloomed among the clumps of cattails.

Sofia scooped up a handful of pebbles and hurled them into the water. Startled frogs scattered as the stones splashed around them. Today had been her chance to prove to Stephanie that she was good at taking care of horses, and she'd totally blown it. She might as well forget about being in Mini Whinnies. She would probably never see Grace or Snickers or Kit Kat again. Her mother's warning rang in her ears. *Don't get too attached.* No, she shouldn't get too attached because every time she did her heart got ripped out of her.

Olivia. Great. She'd promised Olivia to ask if she could join Mini Whinnies, too. Now that would explode in her face. Would Olivia even want to be friends with her anymore? Probably not. Sofia grabbed the biggest rock she could find and slammed it into the pond. Water splashed up, drenching her legs.

A scream rose from deep within her, burning her throat as it burst out. She fell to her knees and sobbed. If only she could go back to live with Gramma Lisa. She missed Sundance more and more each day. Why did Mom take her away from them? It was so unfair.

Mom was in England, having the time of her life with some rich guy Sofia had never even met. What difference did Mom's stupid fight with Gramma Lisa make now that Mom was thousands of miles away? Why couldn't Mom just let go of it?

She should run away from this place. How many miles was it to Connecticut? Probably too far to ride her bike. Maybe she could hitch-hike to Gramma Lisa's house. Or she could wait until Grampy fell asleep and call Gramma Lisa. Her grandmother could drive to Maine and rescue her. Then Sofia could be with Sundance again.

"Sofia!" Grampy's heavy footsteps crashed through the tall grass. "Oh, Sofia, thank God."

Sofia leapt to her feet, teary eyes wide.

"I was so worried. I had no idea where you were. What are you do-ing here?"

"I... I..." Sofia stammered.

"You told me you were helping Stephanie. But she called and said that you left in a big huff. Then you didn't come home."

Sofia wiped her eyes and sniffed. "I'm sorry, Grampy. I didn't think—"

"No, you didn't think, did you," Grampy said. "I don't know what happened at Stephanie's, but I want to make one thing clear to you. From now on, you're not allowed to ride your bike anywhere without my permission."

Sofia kicked at a patch of loose dirt and muttered, "Whatever."

"Put your bike in the back of the car." Grampy's voice sounded stern.

They drove to Grampy's house in silence. As they turned into the driveway, a fresh wave of panic coursed through Sofia's body. A red pick-up truck was parked in front of the garage. Stephanie sat in the driver's seat. Sofia ducked under the dashboard, hoping Stephanie hadn't noticed her.

Grampy opened the car door and climbed out of the driver's seat. Sofia peeked over the window to see Grampy approach Stephanie's truck. Stephanie rolled down her window.

Sofia couldn't hear their conversation and wasn't sure she wanted to. She scrunched her shoulders and squeezed her eyes shut, wishing she had an invisibility cloak like Harry Potter's so she could cover herself and sneak back into the house unseen.

Any minute now, there would be a knock at her window. Grampy or Stephanie would demand that she open the door and face their angry lecture. But the knock never came. Sofia heard the truck's engine start up. Tires crunched on Grampy's driveway. The porch door banged shut.

Sofia trembled, alone in the car. *Grampy must be really mad.*

Chapter 8

Sofia's stomach rumbled. She hadn't eaten breakfast or lunch, and judging from the shadows creeping across the rug, it must be late afternoon. She shifted in her bed and pulled the covers over her ears.

Knock. Knock. Knock.

She stared at the closed door through bleary eyes. "What?"

"You have a visitor," Grampy said.

"Who?"

"Can I come in?" This voice didn't belong to Grampy. It sounded like... Olivia.

What was she doing here? Sofia scrambled out of bed. "Yeah, I guess."

Olivia opened the door and stared at Sofia. "Wow. That's some hairstyle you've got going on there."

Sofia patted down her frizzy hair, but it had a mind of its own. She glanced in the mirror above her dresser. Black ringlets stood at every angle, including straight up.

Olivia giggled. "Oh, I know the feeling. I get unbelievable bed head. But you might want to tidy up a bit. We're taking you out to eat."

"Why are you taking me out to eat?" Sofia asked, suspicious. Did Grampy call Olivia while she was sleeping? What had he told her?

"Because tomorrow is the last day of school, and we always go out to Captain Bob's Boathouse to celebrate. And Mom said I could bring a friend, so I'm bringing you."

Sofia still wore the dirty clothes she had grabbed from her floor that morning. She looked at her reflection a second time. Her face was puffy and dirt stained. "Can I take a shower first?"

"That's okay. No rush. Well, actually, maybe a little rush. Mom and Dad and Ryan are waiting in the van."

Are you kidding me? Sofia grabbed her yellow bathrobe and raced to the bathroom.

***

When they pulled into the large parking lot at Captain Bob's Boathouse, the first thing that caught Sofia's attention was the seagulls. There must have been hundreds of them screeching and swooping down from the roof to fight over the French fries people tossed into the air.

The second thing Sofia noticed was a large wooden statue of a sea-captain. A pair of seagulls perched upon the captain's hat. Bird droppings splattered down the face of the statue, making him look like he was crying white tears.

"I don't recommend ordering the chicken." Ryan snickered. "I hear it's really seagull."

Sofia looked from Ryan to Olivia, unsure about what she might find on the menu.

Olivia poked Ryan in the arm. "Don't listen to him. The food is great here. I'm going to order Bob's Bucket 'O Clams."

Olivia's father, David, held the door open while Pastor Amy, Ryan, and Olivia filed in to the restaurant. Sofia hung back for a moment, took a deep breath, and entered.

"Welcome to Bob's Boathouse." She jumped at the robotic voice to her left. An animatronic fisherman sat on a wooden barrel, its head bobbing and its mouth flapping open and shut out of sync with the words, which were broadcast from a speaker overhead. The mechanical figure held a fishing rod which waved up and down every few seconds.

"That thing totally freaked me out when I was little," Ryan admitted.

"But I loved it," said Olivia. "Wait 'til you see the dancing lobsters."

At that moment, a trio of plastic lobsters reared up on their tails, claws snapping. They flapped and flopped to the sound of wailing electric guitars and drums. One was missing a claw.

"Wah, wah, wah," Ryan shouted as he wildly strummed an imaginary guitar.

Sofia giggled. She liked this silly place.

A tiny woman with deeply tanned skin greeted them and led them to a booth in the corner of the large dining area. Like the other staff, she wore a sailor-like uniform with navy pants, a white shirt, and a short, blue tie.

She handed them menus. "What can I get for you to drink?"

The Murphy family ordered sodas.

Sofia ordered chocolate milk. Her stomach growled loudly. She wished she could crawl under the table.

"Can I get the Fisherman's Platter?" Ryan asked.

Pastor Amy frowned. "I don't know. That's a lot of food for one person. Maybe you should split it."

"Come on, Mom. I'm a growing boy."

"And growing wider by the day," Olivia chimed in.

David glared at his daughter. "Cut it out."

As Sofia examined the menu, she thought she could probably eat an entire Fisherman's Platter by herself. Her mouth watered as she glanced at the fried seafood and French fries piled high on the plates of the nearby diners. "Maybe Ryan and I can spilt one?"

Pastor Amy nodded. "That sounds like an excellent idea, Sofia."

"You can have some of my clams, if you want," Olivia offered.

"Oh no, Olivia. Tell me you aren't ordering an entire bucket of clams." Pastor Amy sighed.

Olivia smiled. "I can share a few with you, if you want, Mom."

"So, Olivia's getting a huge serving of fried clams, but I'm not allowed to get my own fisherman's platter? That's so unfair," Ryan complained, waving his half-finished cup of soda.

"Please," David pleaded. "Let's just have fun tonight. Order what you want, and we can take the rest home for leftovers."

"Or feed it to the seagulls," suggested Olivia.

Pastor Amy buried her face in her hands, muttering to herself.

"Did you ask whether I can join Mini Whinnies?" Olivia asked.

Sofia's body tensed. "Not yet."

"Why not?"

Sofia stared at a ship's wheel mounted on the wall behind Ryan's head and thought for a moment. "Actually, I think I'm going to quit."

"Quit? Why? You sounded so excited about it yesterday."

Sofia wasn't about to tell Olivia and her family what had happened that morning. "'Cause there's not much of a point, since I'm not going to be here much longer. I'm going back to live with my Gramma Lisa soon."

Ryan looked at his father, then at Sofia. "I thought you couldn't go back there because—"

"Ryan." David interrupted.

"Because what?" Sofia felt her face redden.

Ryan glanced back at his father and then down at the menu in front of him. "Oh, nothing. I'm just surprised, that's all. I thought you were going to be here for the whole summer."

A waitress approached their booth. "Hi. My name is Grace and I'll be your server." She paused and smiled. "Hey, Sofia."

Grace was the last person Sofia expected to see. How could her evening get any more awkward? "You work here?"

Grace chuckled. "As a matter of fact, I do. I wear many hats. College student. Horsewoman. And waitress at this fine establishment, to name a few."

"And you used to volunteer at my barn!" Olivia wiggled in her seat. "With the hippotherapy program."

Grace studied Olivia's face. "I didn't even recognize you, Olivia. You've grown up so much. You were such a little firecracker last time I saw you."

"She still is," Pastor Amy added.

"I bet. And Mr. and Mrs. Murphy. It's so nice to see you all."

Ryan cleared his throat dramatically. "I'm Ryan."

"Nice to meet you, Ryan. Now, what would you like to order this evening?"

After Grace took their orders and left the booth, Olivia grabbed Sofia's arm. "I know you aren't going to stay with your Grampy that long, but you can't quit Mini Whinnies. Grace is so awesome. She was the nicest volunteer at my barn. And I'm sure she'd let me join with you. You can ask her when she comes back."

Sofia focused on her empty chocolate milk glass, struggling to come up with a good excuse. "I don't know. Is it okay with your parents? They'd probably have to drive you there and they might be busy."

"Nah, they think it's a great idea, right, Mom?"

Pastor Amy nodded. "As long as it's fine with Grace and her mother. We shouldn't assume anything, Olivia."

"It's gonna be fine. Sofia and I are going to be in the Mini Whinnies together. I just know it."

Sofia swallowed. It wasn't going to be fine, and when Olivia found out, she'd probably whack her in the leg with one of her crutches.

David broke the awkward silence. "Kids, I know you're heart-broken that tomorrow is the last day of school. Ten whole weeks of vacation. I can't imagine what you'll do all day."

To Sofia's relief, Ryan and Olivia launched into a passionate discussion of their summer plans. They were debating which ice cream stand served the best chocolate peanut-butter-cup when Grace arrived with a tray overflowing with fried seafood and French fries.

"Sofia told me about Mini Whinnies, and I want to be in it, too." The words tumbled out of Olivia's mouth so quickly that Sofia wondered if Grace could even understand what she was asking.

"Hmm." Grace winked at Sofia. "That sounds like an excellent idea. Of course, I'll need to check with my mom, first."

Sofia felt heat rise in her cheeks. Did Grace know about this morning's meltdown?

Grace placed an enormous portion of haddock, scallops, shrimp, and clams in front of Ryan, who had ordered his own Fisherman's Platter despite his mother's objection. "And what about you, Ryan? Do you want to be in Mini Whinnies, too?"

Olivia frowned. "Not Ryan. He doesn't even like horses."

"I do, too." Ryan glared at his sister.

"But you're scared of them," Olivia protested.

Grace knelt and looked into Ryan's eyes. "There's nothing wrong with being a little scared. It means that you understand how powerful horses are. Our miniature horses are very well behaved, and because they're so small they aren't as scary as big horses can seem. Would you like to meet them and see how you feel after that?"

Ryan nodded.

Sofia noticed Olivia's balled up fists under the table, and looked away. *If I had a brother, I would be a lot nicer to him.*

***

"Thank you for taking me to dinner." Sofia stepped out of Olivia's van, clutching a large container of leftovers. As it turned out, she couldn't eat an entire Fisherman's Platter after all.

Grampy met her on the porch steps, waving as the Murphy family drove away.

"Stephanie stopped by while you were out. She left you something." He took Sofia's seafood and handed her a small box, wrapped in sparkly blue paper and tied up in a gold ribbon.

Why would Stephanie give her a gift? Her birthday wasn't for a few weeks, and Stephanie was angry at her. It didn't make any sense. Sofia's hands shook as she examined it.

"Open it," Grampy urged.

She untied the ribbon and ran her finger under a flap of the paper, carefully tugging it open. She couldn't tell what was inside.

"I've never seen a kid open a present that slowly. It's not going to bite you. Just rip it off."

Sofia exhaled and tore the paper free. Inside she found a digital alarm clock and a note.

Sofia, ask your Grampy to show you how to set this to 6:00 a.m. That should give you enough time to get to the barn to feed Snickers and Kit Kat their breakfast. See you tomorrow at 6:30. Stephanie.

Chapter 9

Sofia shivered in the early morning fog and wiped cold drizzle from her eyelashes. Despite the dreariness of the day, she had woken a full hour before her new alarm clock beeped at 6 a.m. Unable to fall back asleep, she'd walked in circles around the kitchen and living room, wondering when Grampy would wake. When he finally shuffled out of his bedroom in search of coffee, he insisted that Sofia sit at the table and eat some toast before allowing her to leave at 6:15. Sofia was now glad Grampy had also insisted that she bring her jacket. Summer mornings in Maine could sure be miserable.

As she paced in front of the barn waiting for Stephanie to meet her, Sofia felt as if a moth were flitting around her stomach. Stephanie had given her another chance, and Sofia was determined not to mess things up.

The horses whinnied from inside their stalls. They must have known it was almost feeding time.

A door creaked, and Sofia looked up to see Stephanie walking down her porch steps. She wore a yellow raincoat and electric-blue rubber boots. "Good morning, Sofia. Looks like you beat me to the barn this morning."

Sofia smiled. "Hi."

"Grace wanted to give you a chance to show me what you know," Stephanie said. "She'll come out in a bit."

So this is a test. Sofia's stomach churned.

Stephanie approached the large door at the front of the stable and reached for its handle with both hands. It slid open with a deep groan, and Sofia and Stephanie entered the barn.

Kit Kat's tiny nose peeked over her door. She nickered. In the stall next to her, Snickers snorted and kicked at the wall.

The stall opposite Kit Kat's contained horse-related equipment— a driving cart, harnesses, and an unused saddle that must have once belonged to Toby. The stall across from Snickers was filled with hay bales and bags of wood shavings for the horses' bedding. Sofia followed Stephanie, who pointed to two plastic bins. The cover of one lid was marked "Snickers" and the other "Kit Kat".

Stephanie reached down and unsealed the tightly-fitting lid of Kit Kat's bin. "She gets two cups of this feed. No more, no less." She handed Sofia the cup.

Sofia froze. What if she did it wrong? Taking a quick breath, she measured carefully, scooping the grain into a shallow feed dish. Then she measured a second cup of feed, knocked the excess back into the grain container, and poured it into Kit Kat's bowl. She held it out to Stephanie.

Stephanie nodded. "You can give this to her. Just open the stall door and lay it on the floor."

At Gramma Lisa's barn, Sofia hadn't been allowed to enter the horses' stalls with food. Delilah would lunge at her door, ears pinned, demanding her meal. Even Sundance frightened her with his anxious pacing and insistent whinnies. Heart pounding, Sofia opened the stall door and placed the dish in front of Kit Kat, who thrust her nose into it as if she hadn't eaten for days.

After closing Kit Kat's stall and latching it shut, Sofia returned to the feed area. *That wasn't so bad.*

Stephanie opened Snickers' bin and waved a small scoop in her right hand. "This isn't grain. It's a supplement that gives Snickers the vitamins and minerals he needs without giving him too many calories. This stuff helps maintain proper insulin levels and keeps his hooves healthy. It's very important that you give him the right amount, and that you do not give him any of Kit Kat's grain. Do you understand?"

Sofia nodded, filled the scoop and sprinkled it into the rubber feed dish. She brought the tiny offering to Snickers, who gobbled it up in about fifteen seconds. She wondered if Snickers thought about all the food he wasn't allowed to eat anymore. If she couldn't eat pizza or cookies, she'd probably think about them all the time.

"Good job," Stephanie said. "Now one more thing about the feed. You must always be sure that you close the bins tightly when you finish. Do you know why?"

Sofia remembered last winter, when some rodents took up residence in Gramma Lisa's barn. At first Sofia thought they were cute, and protested when Gramma Lisa set out traps. Then a mouse chewed through Sundance's saddle pad. "You don't want mice to get in?"

"Right. We don't want mice or any kind of creepy-crawlies in their food. So make sure you always put the lid back on nice and tight."

Sofia's next task was to carry armfuls of hay to the horses' paddock. Stephanie showed her how to stuff it into the two hay bags that hung from the fence, one for each horse. If there had been only one place to eat hay, Stephanie explained, Snickers would push his companion away, and wouldn't let Kit Kat eat any. Snickers might be a bully when it came to food, but seeing as he couldn't eat candy or treats anymore, Sofia could forgive him.

After they filled a large water bucket in the paddock and carefully rolled up the hose, Stephanie brought Sofia back into the barn. She smiled and handed Sofia a faded green halter. "Now show me how to put this on Kit Kat."

It's another test, but I know I can do this right.

Kit Kat had finished her breakfast and stood by the stall door, ready for Sofia to slip the halter around her nose. She pulled the crown strap around the back of Kit Kat's ears and fastened the buckle. *Perfect.*

Stephanie nodded and handed a lead rope over the door. "Now lead her out to the paddock."

Sofia clipped the lead rope onto a ring under the nose-piece of Kit Kat's halter. She opened the door, and stepped into the barn aisle, staying on the left side of the tiny chestnut mare.

Gramma Lisa taught her that you should always lead from the horse's left. It was an ancient tradition passed down from the time when knights rode into battle. They carried their swords over their left hip. By working on the horse's left, the sword wouldn't smack into the horse or get caught on its back when people mounted or dismounted. Sofia thought it was kind of silly that this was still a rule hundreds of years later when nobody carried swords anymore, but she wanted to show Stephanie that she knew how to do things correctly.

Kit Kat followed Sofia through the barn and out to the paddock, with Stephanie walking behind.

"Now open the gate and lead her through. Then shut the gate and take off her halter."

Sofia followed Stephanie's directions, pleased she had made no mistakes. Kit Kat trotted to one of the hay bags, and Sofia walked back through the gate and began to walk back to the barn.

"Wait."

Uh oh. Maybe Sofia hadn't done it perfectly, after all.

Stephanie pointed to a metal chain attached to the side of the gate. "I know the gate looks shut. But if one of the horses were to push on it, they could open it easily. So it's very important to wrap this chain around the fence post and back to the gate, and lock it shut every time one of the horses is in here."

"Okay." Sofia repeated the instructions under her breath as she wrapped the chain and clipped it shut.

Sofia and Stephanie returned to the barn. Snickers pawed at the door to his stall.

"Don't get all worked up, Mr. Snickerdoodle. Sofia's going to take you out and then you can stuff your face with hay." Stephanie winked at Sofia and passed her a red halter and matching lead.

As she led the little pinto to his paddock, Sofia wondered why she'd been so afraid of Stephanie. She was strict, but that was because she loved her horses and wanted them to be taken care of the right way. She thought of Sundance, and hoped he was safe and happy.

Sofia rubbed Snickers' neck and kissed him on his tiny nose before removing his halter. She made sure to wrap the chain securely around the gate and lock it before she left.

Grace stood inside the barn, grinning at Sofia, her blonde and purple streaked hair in a tangle. "Hey, Mom. How's the newest member of the Mini Whinnies doing?"

"She's doing a fantastic job. A plus."

"I told you. She knows her stuff." Grace reached for a pitchfork propped against the barn wall. "I'll give her a double A plus if she mucks the stalls for me."

Stephanie laughed. "I don't think you're getting out of your chores that easily, sweetie."

"I don't mind. I'm good at mucking." Sofia hopped from one foot to the other. "I used to muck Sundance's stall every day. And I'll sweep the barn when I'm done."

"How about you do Snickers' stall, and Grace does Kit Kat's. Sweeping will give you extra bonus points," Stephanie replied.

"Oh... extra points, Sofia. Mom must really like you." Grace passed the pitchfork to Sofia. "By the way, Mom, I have a couple of other kids who want to join the club."

Stephanie cocked her head. "Really? So you're serious about starting it back up again."

"Of course! It's no fun having a club with just one member."

Wasn't it two? Grace had told her that she and Sofia would be members together.

"Well, Grace, you're the leader of Mini Whinnies now. I trust your judgment." Stephanie turned to Sofia. "I've got to get ready for work, but you can stay here with Grace if you want. Same time tomorrow?"

"Yes. You can count on me."

As Sofia sifted Snickers' soiled bedding and tossed it into the wheelbarrow, she replayed Grace's words. *Mom must really like you.* Her heart felt so full she could hardly keep from dancing.

Chapter 10

Grace stood beside Kit Kat, motioning for Sofia, Olivia, and Ryan to gather in front of the horse's paddock. Today was the first meeting of the Mini Whinnies Horse Club and Sofia didn't want anything to ruin it. Unfortunately, Olivia hadn't stopped criticizing Ryan since they'd arrived.

Sofia kept her eyes focused on the chestnut mare as they approached the fence. Maybe if she ignored Olivia's negative comments she'd stop making fun of her brother.

Ryan squealed as Grace led Kit Kat through the paddock gate. "She's so adorable!"

"Unlike you," muttered Olivia, scowling.

Grace demonstrated to Ryan how to hold his hand out flat to give Kit Kat a treat. She placed a piece of carrot on his palm. "I promise she won't bite you."

Ryan took a tentative step forward. He towered over the miniature horse, who stretched her nose towards Ryan's waist. As her delicate lips reached for the treat, he squeaked and jumped back.

Olivia snickered.

"It's okay, Ryan." Grace stroked the mare's neck. "She's very gentle."

Ryan reached out his palm a second time. He giggled when Kit Kat took the carrot. "Her lips are so soft." He offered her a second piece of carrot. "She's such a sweetie-pie."

"Why don't you marry her, then." Olivia rolled her eyes and reached across the picnic table to poke Sofia.

Sofia looked away, wishing Olivia would stop tormenting him.

Ryan ignored his sister as he cooed and petted the miniature horse.

Snickers stared at them through the fence. Was he jealous? Sofia resolved to give the pinto several extra hugs before she left. She recognized that Grace wanted to help Ryan get over his fear of horses, but it didn't seem fair to give Kit Kat all the attention, not to mention all the treats. Of course Sofia liked the little mare, but it was Snickers who had stolen her heart.

"So, Ryan, do you think you want to learn how to work with the minis?" Grace asked.

He nodded enthusiastically.

"Great! Then let's get started."

Olivia sat slumped at the picnic table, arms crossed. What was wrong with her this morning?

"Hey there, Miss Firecracker." Grace motioned to Olivia. "Why don't you lead Kit Kat back into her paddock."

Olivia immediately straightened. "Okay."

Sofia's pulse quickened. She didn't want to admit it, but she secretly worried how Olivia's physical limitations might interfere with her work with the horses. How could she lead Kit Kat while depending upon crutches to walk? Pastor Amy insisted on leaving Olivia's wheelchair, but it remained parked beside the barn. And wouldn't the horses be afraid of a wheelchair?

Rising from the picnic table, Olivia repositioned the crutches and made her way toward the mare. Her face softened. "You want to go back in with your little buddy?"

Shifting both crutches into her left hand, she reached for the lead rope with her right. Sofia looked away, not wanting to give the impression she was staring. When she glanced back, Olivia was standing beside Kit Kat, gripping the lead with both hands and leaning on her crutches.

She took a slow but deliberate pace forward and the horse stepped with her. Grace stood close on Kit Kat's other side, apparently ready to assist Olivia, but allowing her to try it by herself. Step by step, the three of them advanced towards the paddock gate.

Sofia didn't realize she'd been holding her breath until it hissed through her teeth. Olivia had removed Kit Kat's halter and was now ambling back through the gate, which she had not locked.

Grace smiled. "Great job, Olivia. Now kids, rule number one of Mini Whinnies is to always close and lock the gate when the horses are inside. We don't want any escapees. Sofia, do you want to show them?"

Sofia jumped from the picnic table and wrapped the chain around the post and the gate, locking it into place before returning to her seat.

"Thanks for showing us rule number one. Why don't we figure out our other rules."

"How about no boys allowed?" Olivia suggested.

"Very funny, sis." Ryan plopped onto the seat beside Sofia.

Grace sat on the other side of the picnic table and picked up a yellow pad of paper. "When I was in Mini Whinnies, my brother and I didn't always get along. But I miss him now. How about rule number two. Respect each other."

Sofia thought that was an excellent rule.

Rules are necessary, but not particularly interesting to talk about, and Sofia appreciated how Grace didn't go on and on about them like some adults would. After a couple of minutes Grace said, "The last rule is 'have fun'. What's the point of being in a horse club if you don't have any fun? So let's talk about some of the things we might do together."

Sofia's hand shot into the air.

Grace laughed. "This isn't school, Sofia. No need for raising your hand. Go ahead."

"You told me when you were in Mini Whinnies you went to horse shows. Can we go to a show?"

Olivia and Ryan murmured enthusiastically.

"I thought you might bring that up," Grace said. "I think that's a great goal. But the three of you will need to learn many new skills first. Participating in a horse show requires preparation."

"We'll work really hard and practice every day." Sofia's words sounded more forceful than she had intended.

"Yes, we will," Olivia agreed.

Grace nodded. "Let's see how it goes. Maybe August. Any other ideas?"

Sofia's hand jumped into the air a second time. It seemed to have a mind of its own. "You said you sometimes brought the horses to parades. Could we march in a parade?"

"That would be awesome," Ryan said. "There's this Fourth of July parade in Ocean Park. They let anyone be in it."

"My mother told me she went to that parade when she was my age." Sofia realized she hadn't thought of her mother in several days. She swallowed and pushed back a surge of guilt.

"I know that parade," Grace said. "Mini Whinnies marched in it when I was about eight or nine. They gave out popsicles to all the participants."

"Yeah, I loved the popsicles." Ryan rubbed his stomach.

Sofia glanced at Olivia, expecting her to make a sarcastic remark. Instead, Olivia appeared to be fascinated by the activities of a pair of ants crawling across the picnic table.

"July Fourth is coming up pretty quickly. Ryan, you'll have to practice handling and leading the horses and develop confidence in your skills." Grace tapped her pen on the yellow pad of paper and gazed into the distance. "Olivia, have you ever driven a horse?"

Olivia lifted her head. "Yeah, I have a few times. Not by myself, though."

"You could help me drive Snickers in the parade. I'd be in the cart with you. How does that sound?"

"Awesome!"

Sofia frowned. Snickers' cart wasn't big enough for all of them to fit. If Grace and Olivia rode in the cart with Snickers, that left Sofia and Ryan with Kit Kat. Was the little mare strong enough to pull them? She closed her eyes, picturing the unoccupied stall containing the harnesses and other equipment. Sofia's heart sank as she realized there was only one cart.

This was so unfair. She'd been getting up at six every morning to help Grace and Stephanie. Olivia wouldn't even have known about the Mini Whinnies if it hadn't been for her.

"Sofia, you have a lot of experience working around horses, but Ryan is just getting started. So I'm hoping you'll be my assistant and help him during the parade. How does that sound?"

It was true that Ryan would need help, but why did she have to be the one to give it? Why not Olivia? Of course it would be a nightmare listening to her bicker with Ryan the entire time. Then the realization hit her like a powerful ocean wave. It would be easy to march in the parade with Ryan and Kit Kat, but walking would be next to impossible for Olivia.

Sofia nodded.

"Great." Grace picked up her pen and twirled it around her fingers. "There's a tradition in Mini Whinnies that my mom started and now I'm passing down to the three of you. Before we do a special trip together, like going to a parade or a horse show, each person needs to learn something new and demonstrate it to the group. You get to pick a topic, research it, and then make a presentation to the others."

"Like an oral report at school?" Ryan asked.

"Yes, kind of like that. But more hands-on." Grace hesitated. "I know what you're thinking. That sounds boring. But you're going to learn a lot."

"I think that sounds fun," Olivia said.

"Really?" Grace sighed, looking relieved. "I mean, yes, it's fun. Sometimes people think the most important thing about working with horses is knowing how to ride. But horses aren't machines. They're living creatures, each with their own personality. So you need to know how to communicate with them and recognize their needs. You're responsible for keeping them safe and healthy, and doing that requires a lot of knowledge and experience."

Grace was right. Sofia loved to ride Sundance. But that was only a small part of their relationship. Even if she never got to ride him again, she would not stop loving him. She wished she could take care of him now, but had confidence that Gramma Lisa was the kind of horse-woman who understood the right way to keep him safe and healthy.

"We have about two and a half weeks before the Fourth of July. We'll meet together every Monday, Wednesday, and Friday, but in be-tween those times I want you to research a topic, learn as much as you can about it, and present it to the group in two weeks. If you all do that, Mini Whinnies will be going to the parade."

"What kind of topic?" Sofia asked.

"I was thinking that you could learn about what to do when your horse is sick. For example, do you know how to take a horse's tempera-ture?"

Sofia tried to imagine sticking a thermometer under a horse's tongue.

Olivia smirked. "I think Ryan should demonstrate how to do that."

Ryan scratched his ear. "Why me?"

Grace attempted to suppress a grin, but Sofia could see that she was about to chuckle. "Oh, Olivia. You won't give your brother a break, will you? I think Olivia should be the one to show us. Just make sure you have a nice, long cord attached to that thermometer."

"No way! That's so gross," Olivia shot back.

"Why?" Sofia didn't understand what all the fuss was about.

"'Cause you have to stick it in the horse's, umm, rear-end." Olivia's face turned even redder than her hair as she choked back laughter. She lost control and snorted.

Ryan doubled over, laughing hard. A moment later, Grace joined them, wiping tears from her eyes.

The giggles overtook Sofia and she fell in a heap on the grass, barely able to breathe. She couldn't wait to see Olivia's demonstration.

Chapter 11

Sofia had left the house wearing her windbreaker, but shed it after leading Kit Kat into the paddock. She dragged an arm across her sweaty forehead and rubbed her stinging eyes. It was seven-thirty in the morning and the large thermometer mounted on the front of the barn already registered eighty-three degrees.

As she pushed an empty wheelbarrow to the barn, Grace emerged from her house, wearing muck boots and pajamas.

Grace yawned. "Good morning. Thanks for doing the chores for me."

"No problem." She looked forward to helping Grace. Giving her friend a few extra minutes of sleep after her late night working at Captain Bob's Boathouse made Sofia feel like she was helping out the big sister she wished she had.

"Boy, it's going to be a scorcher today," Grace said. "I don't think we should work the horses."

"You're not going to make us take the horses' temperatures again, are you?" Thanks to Olivia's comments, it was one of the first things Grace taught them. Witnessing Ryan squeamishly poke the end of a thermometer into Snickers' rear-end was an image Sofia wanted to push out of her brain forever.

Over the past two weeks, the Mini Whinnies had met together six times. Olivia was the first of them to correctly name all the parts of the harness, and was rewarded with the opportunity to drive Snickers at a walk and trot with Grace riding in the cart beside her. Grace let Sofia and Ryan take turns driving Snickers during the next meeting, but Sofia hadn't driven since. She'd willed herself to push back the stab of jealously that crept into her gut every time Olivia and Grace harnessed Snickers. Sofia reminded herself that Olivia couldn't do some of the things she and Ryan could do, like leading the horses over jumps.

The jumps started out as cross-rails, barely six inches in height, but as her confidence grew, Sofia progressed to trotting the horses over two and a half foot obstacles. It would have been easier for Kit Kat to duck under the jumps than over them, but the chestnut mare loved to leap over any obstacle Sofia presented to her. The same could not be said for Snickers, who preferred to skid to a stop in front of the jump and look at Sofia as if she'd just asked him to leap over the moon.

"Earth to Sofia." Grace tapped on Sofia's arm. "I was saying that today would be a good day for the three of you to give your presentations. You're ready, right? I know Olivia is. She's been bragging about it for a week now."

Sofia nodded. She'd wanted to work on her project at the Murphy's house, but Olivia refused, insisting it would spoil the surprise. She made them promise they'd keep their topics top-secret from each other. Unfortunately, Grampy didn't have a computer or an internet connection, and without a cell phone, researching her project required visiting the town library, a building not much bigger than the horses' barn. The librarian enthusiastically showed off their small section on animal care, but Sofia had found most of the information for her report on one of the two computers reserved for their patrons. She really needed a phone. Her birthday was less than two weeks away. Maybe Mom would relent and let her have one now that she was turning eleven.

"I'll give the Murphys a call and let them know that since it's so hot and humid today we're going to do the presentations." Grace trudged back to the house.

An hour later the thermometer had climbed another six degrees. The Mini Whinnies assembled under the shade of the maple tree that towered beside Grace's house. Grace lounged on a beach chair while Sofia and Ryan sprawled on the grass. Olivia sat attentively on a metal folding chair, the only person apparently unaffected by the sweltering weather.

"I call this meeting to order," Grace proclaimed, face solemn. "Today the esteemed members of the Mini Whinnies Horse Club will present their projects. Upon successful completion of their presentations, they will be eligible to participate in the Fourth of July parade."

Olivia tossed both hands into the air like a ballerina and spoke with a silly accent, similar to the one Grace had used. "Honorable leader of the Mini Whinnies, I request permission to present my topic."

"The order of the presentations will be determined through the roll of dice, Miss Murphy." The corners of Grace's mouth twitched. "You may choose two numbers from one through six."

"Three and five. Five is my lucky number," Olivia responded.

Ryan picked a dandelion and tucked it behind his ear. "One, because I'm number one. And two, because, why not?"

"Well, Miss Ruiz, I guess that leaves you numbers four and six." Grace stood, pulled a die from her back pocket and shook it between her hands before letting it fall into her beach chair. "Looks like number two. Ryan, you go first."

Ryan rubbed a hand through the stubble of his sweaty blond hair, dislodging the flower in the process. He grunted as he pushed himself from the grass into a standing position. He reached behind the maple tree and retrieved a large poster-board covered by a black trash bag.

Sofia hadn't thought of making a poster. All she had were some notes she'd scribbled on a piece of paper torn from a spiral-bound pad. Her stomach churned.

"Ladies, brace yourselves. What I am about to show you may be disturbing." Ryan yanked the poster-board free of the trash bag, like a magician sweeping away a cloth to reveal an amazing trick. His poster displayed pasted cut-outs of what appeared to be maggots and bowls of wriggling worms. One featured a highly magnified larva with ridges of spikes encircling its body.

Ryan cocked his head at his silent audience, apparently expecting a stronger reaction from them. "Umm... So these are pictures of parasites. They could be lurking inside one of the horses at this very moment."

He pointed to the picture of reddish, maggoty looking creatures. "These are botfly larvae. You should pay attention, because when I was researching them I found out that sometimes people get the botfly eggs onto their hands, and when they rub their eyes the eggs can get stuck in there. Then they hatch and you have a maggot inside your eyeball and you go blind."

Sofia shuddered.

Olivia wrinkled her nose. "That can't be true. You're making stuff up to gross us out."

"It's true! I read about it and saw pictures and everything."

"Grace, is that really true?" Olivia asked.

"I've never heard of that happening, so I doubt it happens very often. But I guess it could. Anyway, Ryan, why don't you tell us more about horse parasites?"

"Well, as I said, these maggot thingies are called bots. When they grow up they become botflies, which look kind of like bees. In the summer and fall, the botflies lay their eggs on the horse's fur, kind of like how lice stick their eggs in your hair."

Sofia recalled the nightmare in second grade, when she was sent home from school after the nurse did a head check on all the kids in her class. Three of them had lice. Her head itched just thinking about it. She and Mom had been living with her Great Aunt Freda, who freaked out and threw away all of Sofia's stuffed animals and bedding. She cried all night, and in the morning she and Mom moved out. They'd lived in their car for a week before moving in with one of her mother's cousins.

"So the botflies glue their eggs to the horse's legs and belly. Then the horse licks them off and the eggs go inside its mouth. And then they hatch. The larvae hang out in the horse's mouth for four weeks until they grow up a bit. And then it's time for the horse to have nice yummy maggots for dinner. They get swallowed and attach themselves to the horse's digestive tract. They live there all winter, sucking out nutrients from the horse's guts, and then they pupate. You know, like making a kind of cocoon thing so they have a shell around them. And then the horse poops them out."

Sofia felt queasy. Maybe it was the heat, but she didn't think so. She tried to shake the image of squirming maggots from her mind.

"So you've got a pile of horse manure and inside it could be botfly pupae. After a month or two they hatch and become botflies and it all starts again. Which is why our brilliant leader tells us to muck every day."

"You won't get extra points for flattery, Mr. Murphy." Grace smirked. "But good job explaining that for us. I know you researched other parasites, too. Tell us about them."

Ryan grinned like Grace had just handed him a plate of fudge brownies, though hopefully not ones infested with maggots. He pointed to several pictures of worms, explaining that other major horse parasites were tapeworms, lungworms, pinworms, roundworms, and large and small redworms.

"Horses don't get these kinds of worms from flies, though. An infected horse poops out the eggs, and another horse eats from the ground near the poop and the larvae get swallowed. The worms grow inside the horse's intestines or lungs or blood depending on what type of parasite it is, and cause all kinds of damage."

Ryan flipped his poster over, revealing an emaciated horse with random patches of long hair along its belly. Sofia wasn't sure how much more of this she could take. What if Sundance was full of worms and she didn't even know it?

"So, yeah, parasites are really bad. They suck out the nutrition your horse needs and make them look like this. And sometimes they can die."

Olivia raised her hand. "Ryan, I know you're going for the gross-out angle here, so well done and all of that. But they have this stuff called wormer paste. It comes in a tube and you stick down the horse's mouth and the worms die. Goodbye parasites. So, no big deal."

Ryan looked like the imaginary plate of brownies might be crawling with worms after all.

"Actually, it is a big deal," Grace said, "because some of the worms are growing resistant to the medicines we use. Some of them survive and they pass on that resistance to their offspring. We need to be a lot smarter about dealing with parasites now."

Olivia's face reddened.

"So, Olivia, that would make good topic for you to explore this week. Maybe you could present it to us after the parade."

Ryan stifled a laugh. Olivia narrowed her eyes at him.

"Great report, Ryan." Grace clapped while Ryan took a bow.

Grace rolled the dice a second time. "Looks like Olivia's got her lucky five."

Olivia's presentation focused on colic. "It is the leading medical cause of death in horses. In my report, I will tell you about common causes of colic and ways to treat it. Of course, the most important thing is to prevent colic from happening in the first place..."

Sofia felt light-headed. She rubbed her eyes before remembering Ryan's warning about going blind. Every time she closed her eyes she pictured great piles of wriggling maggots.

Her head hurt and her throat felt dry. Her eyes closed again.

Sofia stood in Gramma Lisa's barn, stroking Sundance's golden neck. Sundance yawned, and a fat, red larva wiggled across his tongue. She leapt sideways as wave after wave of maggots streamed from her horse's mouth, filling a bucket by Sundance's feet. The larvae poured out of the bucket, slithered across the floor, and climbed up Sofia's leg. She thrashed wildly as the creatures burrowed under her skin. The maggots were overtaking her, dragging her down, crawling into her mouth and nostrils.

She screamed.

Chapter 12

A hand touched Sofia's shoulder.

"Are you okay?" asked Grace.

"Huh?" Sofia wiped drool from the corner of her mouth.

"I can't believe you're sleeping through my report!" Olivia huffed.

"Let's take a break from Olivia's presentation so you can get some water, okay?" Grace looked concerned.

Sofia nodded. Her legs shook as she stood. Did the others notice? She hoped Olivia wouldn't complain even more about having her speech interrupted.

"Maybe we should call your Grampy," Ryan said. "You don't look so good."

"No, I'm okay. Just really hot." Sofia forced a smile.

A few minutes later, Olivia finished her presentation. No need to roll the dice. It was Sofia's turn now.

She pulled a soggy piece of paper from her back pocket. The blue ink had smudged. A wave of adrenaline coursed through her body, transforming her drowsiness into a jittery blend of nerves and nausea.

Ryan had made a poster. Olivia had apparently memorized enough information to pass a veterinary exam on colic. But what could Sofia offer them? A few scribbled notes? She swallowed hard and introduced her topic.

Laminitis.

"As you already know, Snickers needs a special diet. That's because his body makes too much insulin, which can make it hard to control the level of sugar in his blood. If he eats a lot of sugar he might get laminitis." Sofia glanced at Grace, who smiled and nodded for her to continue.

"I learned that when a word has *itis* after it, it means that it's an inflammation. Like if you have appendicitis, it means that your appendix is inflamed and has to come out. Grampy told me about how that happened to him, how he got very sick had to go to the emergency room."

Sofia closed her eyes in concentration. She'd practiced this part of her report in front of the bathroom mirror at least ten times. "Laminitis is the inflammation of the laminae. The laminae are the tissues that attach the hoof to the rest of the horses' foot. Grace told me it's kind of like the way your fingernail is attached to your finger."

Olivia raised her hand. "So it would be like if the skin under our fingernail got swollen up?"

"Yeah, like that."

Ryan stared at his fingers. "I caught my fingers in the car door once. Boy, did that hurt. One of my fingernails turned black and fell off."

Olivia wrinkled her face. "I remember that."

Sofia wiped her forehead. The sweat stung her eyes. She shook her head and tried to focus. "The laminae have blood vessels running through them. When a horse gets laminitis, the laminae get inflamed. The more they swell, the harder it is for the blood to flow through the vessels. When the blood flow gets cut off, parts of the laminae die. And when that happens, it makes it so they can't glue the hoof and the bone together the way they're supposed to. So yeah, a little bit like Ryan's fingernail, I guess."

Ryan gasped. "Does the hoof just fall off then?"

"I don't think so," Sofia said. "Can it, Grace?"

Grace grimaced. "In very severe cases."

"That's..." Ryan shuddered. "I don't want to think about that."

Neither did Sofia. Another wave of nausea swept over her. She winced, grabbing her stomach.

Grace looked at Sofia. "Are you okay?"

You can get through this. You know this. Sofia nodded and tried to smile.

"Okay." Grace looked uncertain. "Just tell us what you learned."

"I learned that when parts of the laminae die, the coffin bone can start to slip out of place. Once that happens, it can never go back to normal. The horse might be permanently lame. And sometimes the best thing is to put the horse to sleep so it won't be in pain for the rest of its life."

"Wait, but didn't Snickers get laminitis before?" asked Ryan.

"He did," Grace answered. "But we caught it early enough, before there was serious damage to his hooves."

"He was lucky," Olivia said. "A horse at my barn got it. He couldn't even walk. They had to call the vet to put him down."

Grace nodded. "Many horses die from it. Even famous racehorses like Secretariat and Barbaro."

Sofia felt dizzy. She didn't know how much longer she could keep talking.

Grace stretched and yawned. "It sure is hot. Let's try and wrap this up. So Sofia, can you tell us how to check for signs of laminitis?"

"Check for heat in the hooves and feel for a pounding heartbeat in the lower part of the leg." Sofia couldn't find the words to explain it. She frowned. The report sounded much better in front of the mirror. "And see if the horse is standing funny, trying to take the weight off his front feet. It looks kind of like a rocking horse."

"So, how can we help Snickers not to get laminitis?" Grace prompted.

Olivia raised her hand. "I know! Don't let him eat grass. Because the sugar can make him get laminitis, right?"

"That's true," said Grace. "And because he's had it once, he's more likely to develop it in the future."

Sofia needed to sit. She had spent several hours researching this topic, but her brain felt fuzzy, and the facts kept sliding around in her mind. She remembered reading something about standing a horse in ice water to slow down the swelling, but she didn't have the energy to utter another word.

"So let's give Sofia a round of applause for her report." Grace began to clap.

Ryan and Olivia joined in.

"At our next meeting, we'll plan for the parade." Grace stood, wiping her palm across her forehead. "But I need to get ready for work. You three should sit in the shade until Mr. Richardson comes to pick you up."

Sofia drained the rest of her glass of water and closed her eyes.

***

"Where is your Grampy?" Olivia grumbled. "He's twenty minutes late already."

Sofia didn't know. She felt like her mind had detached from her body and was drifting somewhere over the miniature horses' paddock. Or maybe it was floating by the maple tree, still feebly attempting to give a report on the causes of laminitis.

"Does the air conditioner in your Grampy's car work?" asked Ryan. "My dad's too cheap to get ours fixed."

"Yeah, thank God." Sofia had tried to call Grampy from Grace's phone, but there'd been a busy signal. It wasn't like him to be late. *Where is he?*

Grace's hair was still wet from the shower she managed to slip in after their Mini Whinnies meeting. She had changed her clothes and now stood beside her vehicle, jiggling her keys and frowning. "Sorry, kids. I really have to go to work now."

She climbed into the small, green car and started the engine. A moment later she rolled down the window. "You should probably just walk back to Sofia's house, okay? Or maybe I should drive you?"

"There's Mr. Richardson." Ryan pointed as Grampy's old Subaru turned into the driveway.

"Great! See you soon." Grace waved as she drove away.

"Grampy. You're late." Sofia realized she was being rude, but she felt too miserable to care. She wished she could dump a bucket of ice water over head.

"Your mother called just as I was getting ready to pick you up."

"Oh." She wiped beads of sweat from her forehead. *What does she want?*

Olivia opened the front, passenger-side door. "Shot gun!"

"No fair," Ryan muttered as he climbed into the back seat.

Sofia was about to join him when she remembered that she'd left her windbreaker hanging on a post in the minis' paddock. It seemed ridiculous that she'd brought a jacket to the barn today. It had been too warm for one even at six-thirty in the morning. But if she left it hanging there all night, she'd probably get an earful from Stephanie tomorrow.

"Just a minute. I have to get my jacket." Sofia trudged towards the gate. She felt like she'd just stepped off a Tilt-a-Whirl. The world began to spin and the ground rose to meet her.

"Sofia!" Grampy shouted.

Ryan jumped out of the car. "What happened? Did you trip?"

Sofia mumbled. Her words weren't coming out the right way.

Grampy's arms were around her, lifting her.

"I'll get your jacket." Ryan sounded like he was speaking to her from underwater.

Dark spots swam across her vision before the blackness overtook her.

Chapter 13

Sofia stared at the brown water stain on the ceiling of her bedroom. It looked like a panting dog with an extra long tongue lolling from its mouth. Her sweaty socks, t-shirt, and jeans lay in a crumpled wad at the end of the bed. Olivia sat beside her, wiping a cold washcloth over Sofia's forehead.

Someone rapped on the door. Sofia snatched at her sheet and drew it over her body.

Ryan's voice was muffled by the loud humming of Grampy's air conditioner. "Mr. Richardson told me to bring Sofia some water."

"You can't come in. She's in her underwear," Olivia said matter-of-factly. "I'll come to the door. You can give me the water, but you have to promise to close your eyes."

Ryan laughed. "I promise."

Sofia felt her face grow even hotter. She couldn't imagine how this day could get any more embarrassing. At least she'd been able to talk Grampy out of rushing her to the hospital, insisting that she just felt a bit woozy from the heat. He told her that if she wasn't better in half an hour he would take her whether she wanted to go or not.

Olivia retrieved the glass of water and held it out to Sofia. "Can you sit up?"

"Of course I can." Sofia's head pounded, but she no longer felt dizzy. She took a sip of water.

"Come on. Drink it all."

Olivia sounded like her mother. *Oh no. Please, Grampy, do not call Mom.*

Sofia looked at the ball of sweaty clothes at the end of the bed. She couldn't just hang out in her underwear all day. She reached for her jeans.

Olivia shook her head. "Why are you putting those back on? I can get you some shorts. Just tell me where they are."

"They're dirty," Sofia muttered.

"Well, so are those jeans. Who cares if they're dirty? At least you'll be cooler."

Yes, this day could get more embarrassing after all. The truth was Sofia only had one pair of shorts, and they were about two sizes too small. Most of her summer clothes had been left at Gramma Lisa's house, forgotten in her mother's haste to move Sofia out. Mom had promised to replace them as soon as she saved up some money. If her new boyfriend Paul really lived in a castle in England, he must be loaded with cash, but that wouldn't help Sofia now. Grampy hadn't seemed to notice her scant wardrobe, and she couldn't imagine going clothes shopping with an eighty-year-old man, even if he had.

"I'll just put these on." Sofia picked up her damp jeans.

Olivia grabbed a pant leg. "No, you won't. It's too hot. Do you want your Grampy to call the ambulance?"

Now *that* would be embarrassing.

"Do you promise not to laugh?" Sofia asked.

"Why would I laugh at you wearing shorts? Do you have hairy legs or something?" Olivia peered at Sofia's bare legs.

"No." She tugged the sheet back over her legs.

"Sorry." Olivia shrugged. "See, I have hairy legs, but luckily nobody notices because they're too busy staring at my fancy leg-braces instead."

Sofia wasn't sure if she should smile, but she couldn't help it.

"I know," Olivia said, "You have totally dorky pink and blue polka-dotted shorts and you don't want Ryan to be jealous."

Sofia giggled.

Olivia grinned at her.

"My shorts are too small for me," Sofia admitted.

"Oh. Some girls like to wear short shorts. But I guess that's not your style, is it?"

"Not really."

Olivia scratched the back of her head. "This calls for a shopping spree."

Sofia stared at the floor and mumbled, "I don't have any money."

"Well, I've got ten dollars." Olivia patted her pocket. "It isn't much, but I bet we can find a couple of pairs of shorts at Goodwill. Maybe even a cute top to go with them. Do you think your Grampy will take us? If you're feeling better, that is."

Sofia shook her head. "I can't take your money."

"Don't be stupid." Olivia poked Sofia's shoulder. "We've got some shopping to do."

***

"You're getting over heat-stroke. I should take you to the doctor, not the mall," Grampy insisted.

"It was nothing." Sofia took a sip of water. "I'm drinking lots of water, and I feel fine now."

Grampy pursed his lips and shook his head.

"See, Mr. Richardson, the reason why Sofia got so hot was because she doesn't have any shorts." Olivia reached into her pocket and pulled out her ten dollar bill. "If we go to Goodwill, I can buy her some. And that way, she won't get heat-stroke again."

"That is very kind of you, Olivia, but it's not necessary." Grampy turned to Sofia. "Why didn't you tell me you needed clothes? I would have been happy to buy you whatever you needed."

Sofia shrugged. She didn't want Grampy to have to spend a lot of money on her.

Grampy sighed. "If you're still feeling okay this afternoon, I'll take you. But no more outside activities in this heat."

***

Sofia didn't know the first thing about fashion, but Olivia insisted that even a horse-girl needed a few cute outfits. Olivia picked out shorts and tops and even a few dresses that she said would look perfect on Sofia. As she tried on each item of clothing, her friend oohed and aahed as if she were a famous model.

She followed Olivia, pushing her half-filled shopping cart through the thrift shop. They spotted Ryan in a corner behind the men's shoes.

"Look at this!" Ryan plopped an oversized, fuzzy, top hat onto Olivia's head. Red and white stripes rose from a blue base, encircled with white stars. "It would be perfect for the Fourth of July parade. And it's only two bucks."

Sofia nodded enthusiastically. It was a pretty awesome hat. "We should get things to dress up the horses for the parade."

"That's what I was thinking." Ryan pointed to the next aisle. "When you and Olivia were trying on clothes, I noticed there's a whole section of stuff we can use for decorating."

Olivia examined a roll of crepe paper. "I think we should decorate the cart with red, white, and blue streamers."

Sofia picked up a spool of patriotic-themed ribbon. "Maybe we could braid their manes and tails with this."

"And the horses could wear these around their necks." Ryan pointed to some bandanas that looked like the American flag.

Grampy wandered into the aisle, cradling a stack of old books. "So, did you find everything you wanted?" He examined Sofia's cart. "We can go somewhere else if you need to."

"No, Grampy. I'm all set. Really."

Grampy shuffled the books into one arm and picked up the hat. "Hmm." He placed it on Sofia's head.

"That's Ryan's. For the parade," Sofia said.

"I'll pay for it, Mr. Richardson." Ryan took the hat.

"No need. It's on me," Grampy said. "Let's finish up here and I'll take you out for ice cream."

***

Ryan wiped off his chocolate mustache with the back of his hand. "Thanks for treating us, Mr. Richardson."

"You're welcome, young man."

Sofia rested her head on her hands. A paper napkin skittered across the picnic table, fluttering into her face. She batted it away.

"Looks like we're finishing up just in time." Olivia gestured at an ominous cloud darkening the afternoon sky. Thunder rumbled in the distance.

They climbed into Grampy's car. Sofia hesitated before buckling her seat-belt.

"Can we stop at the horses?" Sofia asked. "I'm kind of worried about them. They're outside and there's a storm coming."

"I'm sure they'll be fine," Grampy said. "Stephanie and Grace have things under control."

Sofia bit her lip. "Yeah, but they're not home."

Olivia nodded. "It wouldn't hurt to check, would it? We left them outside. Shouldn't we bring them back to their stalls?"

Grampy started the engine. "I don't want you three out during a thunderstorm. If the storm gets too close, I want you back in the car. One big scare is enough for the day."

As they turned down Stephanie's driveway, a white streak sliced across the sky. Sofia counted. One. Two. Three. Four. Five. Six. Boom! The lightning was still more than a mile away.

She jumped out of the car. A fat raindrop splattered on her nose. She scanned the paddock, looking for Snickers and Kit Kat.

Olivia stepped out of the Subaru. "Where are the horses? Do you think someone brought them in already?"

"I'll check." Ryan ran towards the barn. A moment later, he sprinted out, panic in his voice. "They aren't in there."

Sofia's heart began to race. Had someone stolen the horses?

Ryan dashed to the paddock. "The chain isn't around the gate. It isn't locked."

"There they are!" Olivia pointed to the steep hill behind the barn. "They're way up on the top, next to the tree line."

Grampy rolled down the driver's side window. "What's wrong?"

Sofia fought against the wave of panic rising within her gut. "The horses are loose. Someone must not have shut the gate."

Olivia's eyes narrowed and her glare fell upon her twin. "Ryan. You were the last one to go through the gate."

"What? It wasn't me," Ryan shot back.

"Remember. You got Sofia's jacket." Olivia pointed a crutch at Ryan. "You idiot. Lock the gate. It's the first rule of the Mini Whinnies."

Ryan stomped his foot. "I'm not an idiot. Everything was totally crazy! Sofia passed out. It's not my fault."

"Yes, it is!"

"Stop it!" Sofia shouted, hoping to be heard over their growing argument. "There's no time for fighting. We have to catch the horses right now, before the storm comes."

Then a horrible realization washed across her, churning her stomach with dread. Green grass. How long had Snickers been eating the grass? She remembered her laminitis report. It might already be too late.

Chapter 14

"Hurry! We have to catch the horses." Sofia ran into the barn and grabbed the halters and lead ropes from their stall doors. Heart hammering, she sprinted back outside and threw one to Ryan. "You get Kit Kat, and I'll get Snickers."

"Why Ryan? What about me?" Olivia demanded.

Sofia stared at her in disbelief. The horses stood at the top of a steep hill, over a hundred yards away. It would probably take Olivia several minutes to reach them. Another streak of lighting spilt the darkened sky. She didn't have time to deal with Olivia's drama right now. "We need to get the horses into the barn as fast as possible. You and Grampy should call Grace and Stephanie."

"How? We don't have phones," Olivia said. "And they don't have a landline in the barn."

"You'll have to call from Grampy's house." She wasn't sure if they even had phone numbers for Stephanie or Grace. Where did Stephanie work? She had never thought to ask. At least she knew where Grace was. Maybe Grampy could call Captain Bob's Boathouse and ask for her.

Sofia rushed to the car. "Grampy, it's an emergency. You and Olivia need to go home and call Grace and Stephanie. Ryan and I have to catch the horses."

Grampy opened the door. "I can't leave you and Ryan alone. It's too dangerous."

Sofia didn't have time for arguing. Every moment they stood there doing nothing brought Snickers a step closer to becoming painfully lame or worse. She didn't want to disobey, but she had no other option. "Sorry. I have to get Snickers."

Ignoring Grampy's protest, she turned and raced up the hill.

Ryan followed.

Huge raindrops splashed on Sofia's head and arms as she fought her way through a tangle of weeds and knee-high grass. She stumbled over an unseen rock, staggering to catch her balance.

"Are you okay?" shouted Ryan, slowing as he passed her. They had almost reached Kit Kat.

"I'm fine." Sofia paused for a moment, making sure that Ryan slipped the halter around the mare's nose before sprinting toward Snickers.

As Sofia approached, the pinto jumped and whirled sideways. *Slow down. Don't scare him.* Sofia took a deep breath and exhaled. "Good boy, Snickers."

She took a step towards the startled horse. "It's okay, boy." Another step. With the halter in her left hand, she reached her right arm towards Snickers' head. One more step and she'd be there.

Crack. BOOM! The ground beneath her feet shook. Snickers snorted and leapt out of Sofia's grasp.

Sofia clutched at the air. "No, Snickers!"

The horse bolted towards the woods.

"Help!"

Sofia spun around. Ryan struggled to hold Kit Kat, who strained against her lead rope, the whites of her eyes showing.

"Whoa. Whoa!" Ryan pleaded, fighting to prevent the mare from escaping his grasp. Kit Kat reared, front legs thrashing wildly. Ryan squeaked and tumbled backward, the lead slipping through his fingers. Now free, the terrified mare galloped after Snickers.

"I didn't mean to let go," gasped Ryan as he scrambled to his feet. "I'm sorry."

Another rumble of thunder drowned out Ryan's words. The rain came in sheets now, soaking Sofia's jeans and tee-shirt. The wind lashed at her hair and stung her eyes, making it difficult for her to see, but she couldn't lose track of the horses. *Please don't get lost in the woods.* She trembled as panic threatened to overtake her. *Please don't run into the road and get hit by a car.*

Sofia leapt forward, preparing to chase after the horses. *Wait.* Something in the back of her mind commanded her to stop, to think. She couldn't outrun Kit Kat and Snickers, and chasing them would only drive them away. She needed to be calm. How could they catch the horses and bring them back to the barn?

Then it came to her. Peppermints. She remembered the day she met Grace. Hadn't she said Snickers would do anything for a peppermint? Even the sound of a crinkling wrapper would be enough to make him jump through a ring of fire. Grace had probably been exaggerating, but it was worth a try.

Ryan sniffed and wiped his face. Was it the rain? Or was he crying? Sofia couldn't tell.

"I have an idea," she said. "What if we try peppermints? Grampy has a stash of them in his glove compartment."

Ryan nodded, but appeared unconvinced. "You know more about horses than I do."

They jogged down the hill. Sofia's waterlogged sneakers squished with each step.

Olivia and Grampy stood beside the barn, soaked from the downpour. What were they doing out there? They needed to call Stephanie and Grace.

"Why did you guys let go of them?" Olivia demanded.

Sofia chose to ignore Olivia. It was the look on Grampy's face that worried her.

Grampy reached for Sofia's hand. "It isn't safe. Leave the horses. They'll come back to the barn on their own."

"Please, Grampy. Remember what I told you when I was working on my report? Snickers is in trouble." Sofia held Grampy's hand and looked up to his wrinkled face, willing him to understand. "It's our fault that they got out in the first place. I know we can catch them. I want to try and lure Snickers with one of your peppermints, okay?"

"Will that work?" Grampy asked.

"Actually, that's not a bad idea," Olivia said. "But it might be even better if you got a bucket and filled it with some grain and shook it to get their attention. I saw someone do that once at the barn where I ride."

Sofia shook her head. "Snickers can't eat grain."

"Well, he can't eat peppermints, either, so what's the difference?"

Of course, Olivia's right. "Okay. Maybe we should try both. Ryan can shake the bucket and I'll take the peppermints."

"I'll go get it." Ryan darted into the barn.

"Grampy, please don't wait any longer. You need to call Stephanie. Or Grace," Sofia pleaded.

"Not until I know you're safe inside."

Sofia sighed and walked to the car. She grabbed every one of Grampy's peppermints and shoved them into her pocket.

A moment later, Ryan reappeared, clutching a small bucket. "Ready?"

Sofia nodded. "We need to act calm. Otherwise they might just run away from us again." Sofia did not feel calm. She felt like throwing up. *But Snickers needs me.*

As they reached the top of the hill, Sofia spotted the horses huddling under a huge pine tree.

Ryan began to rattle the container of grain, shaking it from side to side. Kit Kat's ears pricked forward. She nickered and took a step toward Ryan.

"Good girl. Come and get it." Ryan shook the bucket again.

Snickers eyed Sofia before reaching for another mouthful of grass.

Sofia pulled out a peppermint candy and held it in front of her. "Look at what I've got for you." She crinkled the wrapper, hoping he could hear it over the pounding rain.

Ryan's triumphant voice cried out, "I've got her!" He stood beside Kit Kat, stroking her neck and offering her a mouthful of grain.

"Come on, Snickers. I know you want this." Sofia cautiously approached the miniature horse, holding out the peppermint. He snorted. Sofia held her breath. Then he stepped toward her. Another step. And another. Almost there.

Snickers' velvety lips stretched forward, reaching for the peppermint. He really wanted that treat. She would have to trick him, though. It was bad enough that he'd been eating grass. She wasn't about to give him candy.

Sofia crinkled the wrapper again and looped the lead rope around his neck to hold him in case he tried to run. She carefully slipped the halter around Snickers' nose, pulled the nylon strap behind his ears and buckled it securely. The gelding nudged her hand.

"I'm sorry. You can't have it." Sofia shoved the candy into her pocket.

Snickers eyed her pocket, but didn't protest.

As she led him back down the hill, a new wave of dread washed over Sofia. He didn't seem to be lame— yet. But Sofia knew from her laminitis report that the sugar from the grass he ate might produce dangerous toxins in his stomach. These poisons could travel in his bloodstream to the laminae, causing the sensitive tissue surrounding his hooves to heat up and swell. If that happened, Snickers would be in so much pain that he could barely walk. He might never recover.

Grampy stood just inside the barn door. He called out to her, "Thank God, you're okay."

"What can I do?" Olivia shouted over the rain.

Itis meant swelling. Sofia remembered reading that ice could prevent or slow down swelling. "Can you try and find some buckets? The bigger the better. We need to fill them with ice water and cool down his feet."

Olivia nodded. "Good idea."

"Grampy, do we have any bags of ice? We need as much as we can get."

Grampy paced inside the barn. "I don't want to leave you."

"It's an emergency!" shouted Sofia. "We need to get ice, and we need to call Grace and Stephanie."

Grampy frowned and stared at the ground for a moment. "Get inside. And stay safe. I'll be back as soon as I can."

Sofia led Snickers into the barn and halted him in the center aisle. Ryan had already brought Kit Kat into her stall and was latching her door.

What if Kit Kat got laminitis from eating the grass? It didn't seem likely, but... "I think we should check her feet, too."

Olivia appeared with a large plastic bucket. "I remember what you said in your report. Check for heat in the hooves. I can check Kit Kat, and Ryan can fill this with cold water. There's another bucket in that empty stall."

Sofia bent to touch Snickers front feet. They were wet. But were they warmer than normal? She wasn't sure.

"I think she's fine," Olivia called from inside Kit Kat's stall. "Didn't you say something about taking their pulse from above the hoof?"

That's right. Feel for a digital pulse. But how do you do that? Sofia squeezed her eyes shut and tried to imagine the picture she'd seen on the computer screen at the library. "Put your fingers on the sides of her leg, a little above the hoof. Just above that bumpy part. The, umm... I think it is called the fetlock. Do you know where that is?"

"Of course I do. I memorized all the parts of the horse when I was seven."

This fact did not surprise Sofia.

"If you feel a strong pulse, that's bad. If you don't feel anything, that's good." Sofia ran her fingers down the sides of Snickers' foreleg to just above the fetlock. She couldn't feel anything, but she wasn't sure if that was because Snickers didn't have what the website had called a "bounding pulse", or because she didn't know what she was doing. She feared that it was the latter.

"Where do you want the water buckets?" Ryan dragged a heavy container over the wooden floor.

"You can leave it there and put the second one next to it." Sofia directed Snickers to the bucket. He sniffed the water and took a drink.

"Don't drink it, silly. You have to put your feet in it." She picked up the gelding's front left leg and guided it into the water.

Snickers lifted it back out.

"No. In." Sofia gently lifted his leg.

This time he stood.

"Good boy. Now this one." She reached for his right leg and placed that into the plastic bucket. The water reached half-way to his knees.

Ryan dragged the second bucket and tried to position it under Snickers' belly.

Sofia feared that Snickers would spook, but other than shifting his hindquarters, the horse remained steady. Getting his hind legs actually into the water proved more challenging. After three unsuccessful attempts, Snickers knocked over the bucket and a torrent of water streamed down the barn aisle.

Ryan grabbed the container and righted it. "Do you think I should refill it?"

"Obviously," Olivia said.

"What is going on in here?" Stephanie stood in the doorway, hands on her hips, mouth tight. "I see you brought the horses in, which I appreciate, but what are you three doing in here without an adult?"

Olivia pointed at her twin. "Ryan left the gate unlocked, and the horses got out."

Stephanie glared at Ryan, who crouched over the bucket, frozen in place. Then her eyes widened. "How long have they been out?"

Sofia's voice quavered. "We don't know."

Chapter 15

Stephanie rushed towards Snickers and ran her hand down one of his front legs, lifting it out of the bucket of cold water. "Is he lame?"

Sofia shook her head. She would be kicked out of Mini Whinnies for sure. Stephanie might never allow her on her property again, and she wouldn't blame her. After all, it was their fault Snickers had escaped. Ryan forgot to lock the gate, but that wouldn't have happened if she hadn't left her jacket in the paddock in the first place. If someone ever did something stupid to hurt Sundance... Sofia didn't even want to consider what she'd do.

"Was this your idea?" Stephanie pointed to the bucket.

Sofia hung her head and nodded.

Stephanie dipped her finger into the water. "You're trying to cool his feet?"

Sofia looked up. "Yes."

"That's a great idea."

"It is?" Her heart beat faster. Maybe she wouldn't be kicked out of Mini Whinnies after all.

"It's a brilliant idea," Olivia said. "And Mr. Richardson's getting ice so the water can be cooler. It'll stop that laminitis right in its tracks."

"Hmm." Stephanie repositioned Snickers' leg and brushed her hand through his mane. "That makes sense. Keeping his feet cool might prevent swelling."

Olivia winked at Sofia. "She's a real expert on laminitis. She had us check the horses' hooves to see if they were hot. We checked for a digital pulse, too. We didn't feel anything out of the ordinary."

"Good thinking," Stephanie said. She turned to Ryan. "Can you fill this back up with water?"

Ryan jumped to his feet and grabbed the overturned bucket.

"Once it's filled, we'll get Snickers' hind legs into the bucket. Then I'll call Dr. Collins."

***

A ray of brilliant sunshine burst through a gap in the clouds as Dr. Collins' cargo van crunched over the gravel driveway. Sofia jumped up from the picnic table, where she and Olivia had been waiting anxiously, and poked her head through the barn door.

Grampy and Ryan sat beside each other on a hay bale, engrossed in a conversation about the Red Sox. At least that's what they'd been discussing when Olivia had convinced Sofia that they should go outside for a few minutes to "get some fresh air." The barn remained hot and stuffy, and Sofia suspected that her friend was worried that she might collapse from heat-stroke at any moment, even though Sofia insisted she was just fine.

Grace stood by Snickers' side, gripping his lead rope as his feet continued to soak in the ice water.

"He's here," Sofia said. "Finally."

Stephanie followed her to the veterinarian's van.

Dr. Collins flicked mud from his green coveralls before extending a hand toward Stephanie. "I was dealing with a nasty colic. This heat did a number on Tom Johnston's old mare."

"Thanks for getting here when you could. I know it's late and you probably want to get home for dinner," Stephanie said.

Sofia wondered if Dr. Collins frequently worked late, because it looked like he missed a lot of dinners. He was a short, rail-thin man, only a few inches taller than Sofia. Wild tuffs of grey hair poked out from every direction. He looked like he hadn't brushed it in some time.

"So, your mini got into the grass and he's got a history of laminitis? Let's take a look." Dr. Collins hoisted a large, plastic container from the back of his van.

Sofia hopped over a puddle, landing beside him. More mud splashed onto his coveralls. "Can I help carry anything?"

"Oh." The vet seemed to notice her for the first time. "And who are you?"

"This is Sofia." Stephanie put her hand on Sofia's shoulder. "She had the presence of mind to check on the horses during the thunderstorm, and discovered they were loose. She and her friends brought them safely into the barn. And she knew to check their feet for heat and for a bounding pulse."

"You must have taught her well," Dr. Collins said.

"No. She learned this on her own." Stephanie squeezed Sofia's shoulder. "When I got home, she had Snickers standing in cold water."

Dr. Collins cocked his head at Sofia. "Quite impressive, young lady. There've been some recent studies that have demonstrated that cooling a horse's feet can be effective in preventing the onset of acute laminitis. Yes, quite promising. We must be reading the same journals."

"Which journals do you read, Dr. Collins?" Olivia asked.

Sofia hadn't noticed Olivia approaching them. Neither had Dr. Collins, apparently.

"Another one? Who are you?"

"Olivia. Nice to meet you." She held out her hand.

The vet stared at Olivia's outstretched hand for a moment, before seeming to realize that he should shake it. "Okay, then. Let's take a look at the horse."

Dr. Collins turned away from Olivia and Sofia and followed Stephanie into the barn.

"Do you really read vet journals?" asked Sofia.

Olivia shrugged. "When I was researching colic. You know, for the presentation you slept through this morning."

"I wasn't feeling—"

"I'm just teasing you." Olivia grinned. "Come on, let's see what Dr. Collins has to say about Snickers."

Dr. Collins dug a stethoscope from the jumble of instruments in his box. He placed the round part in the area in between Snickers' left front leg and belly and listened. "Heart rate is 38. Respiration is normal."

"That's good," Olivia whispered to Sofia. "If it's high, it can mean that the horse is in pain."

"He needs to step out of those buckets so I can check him for signs of lameness," Dr. Collins said to Grace.

After running his hands down each of Snickers' legs and poking his finger around the top of his hooves, the vet reached for a metal tool that Sofia had never seen before. It looked like giant, long-handled pincers. Dr. Collins picked up one of Snickers' feet and squeezed his hoof with the instrument.

"Don't hurt him," Sofia blurted before she could stop herself.

The vet grunted, but didn't look up. "I've been a vet for thirty-five years. I know what I'm doing, young lady."

Sofia flinched. Her throat burned and her eyes began to water.

Olivia scrunched up her face and stared at Dr. Collins' backside. Sofia had seen that look before. Her friend was on the verge of another one of her dramatic outbursts.

Grace's eyes darted from Sofia to Olivia before settling on the veterinarian. "He's using hoof testers. It's part of an exam for lameness. He's squeezing different sections of Snickers' hooves to see if there are any places that are sensitive to the pressure."

Olivia nudged Sofia, pointed to Dr. Collins, and rolled her eyes. "Want to get some fresh air, again?"

Sofia didn't want to leave Snickers, but she nodded and followed Olivia outside.

"Nice bedside manner," Olivia muttered. "Are you okay?"

"Yeah, I guess so." Sofia swallowed hard. Just a few minutes ago, she felt like a hero— the girl who had saved Snickers through her quick thinking. Stephanie had been so proud of her. Now she felt like an ignorant little kid. She should have kept her mouth shut.

"I didn't like the way he jumped down your throat," Olivia said. "He could've just explained it the way Grace did."

"Did you know what those things were?" Sofia asked.

"Well, yeah. But still. They look like you could use them for a medieval torture device."

"I'm such an idiot." Sofia kicked the dirt.

"No you're not! You were the one to think of using the ice water, and that was really smart. Dr. Collins even thought so."

Sofia sighed. "You know something? I think you'd be a great vet. You know so much about taking care of horses."

Olivia frowned and fidgeted with the Velcro strap that wrapped under her knee.

"Did I say something wrong?"

"No. It's just...I've always wanted to be a vet. Ever since I was about six years old. But that's never gonna happen." Olivia tapped the hard plastic brace supporting the back of her calf.

Sofia remembered something Mom always told her. "You can do whatever you want if you try hard enough." Even as she said it, she wondered if that was really true.

"No offense, but that's a bunch of baloney. Who's going to want a vet who looks like me? Would you? A big horse could push me right over. Can you picture me trying to use hoof testers on a draft horse?"

Sofia couldn't. Dr. Collins had placed Snickers' hoof between his legs and used both hands to squeeze. She didn't think Olivia could keep her balance doing that, and she wouldn't be strong enough to hold the hoof of a misbehaving horse. "But you're so smart. Maybe if you had an assistant. Hey, I could be your assistant!"

Olivia offered a half-smile. "Sounds like a plan."

Just then, Ryan and Snickers walked through the barn door.

Dr. Collins followed, writing something on a clipboard. "I want you to trot him down the driveway about twenty-five feet, then turn and trot back."

Ryan clutched the lead rope. "Come on, buddy, let's go." He urged Snickers into a steady trot.

Dr. Collins watched the gelding's movement. "I don't see any signs of unsoundness. Okay, you can trot him back to me."

Olivia scowled.

"Did the vet do something wrong?" Sofia asked.

"No. It's just so unfair."

"What do you mean?"

"Ryan. A couple weeks ago, he was scared to death of horses. Now look at him."

"Yeah, he's learned a lot, hasn't he?" Sofia didn't understand why this was unfair. If anything, Olivia was often unfair to her brother.

Olivia pounded the grass with one of her crutches. "You don't get it, do you?" She turned her back on Sofia. "Nobody ever does."

Chapter 16

Pastor Amy stacked three large pizza boxes on the picnic table beside the minis' paddock.

"Hey, Ryan! Mom's here, and she brought us pizza," Olivia yelled to her twin, who was still inside the barn with Snickers and Dr. Collins.

A moment later, Ryan burst through the barn door. "Mom, you're the best. I'm starving." He reached for the top box and began to lift the cover.

"Your hands are filthy," Pastor Amy said. "Go wash them."

Ryan groaned. "You guys better not eat all the pepperoni."

"They're going to wash their hands, too, aren't you girls?" Pastor Amy pushed Olivia's hand away from the pizza.

Sofia, who'd been about to pour herself some root beer, quickly shoved her hands into her pockets.

Grampy wandered over to the table and reached into a bag of barbecue-flavored chips. He hadn't washed his hands, but Pastor Amy said nothing.

After a visit inside Stephanie's house, Sofia and Olivia returned to the picnic table. Ryan shoved the last remnants of what Sofia assumed was his first slice of pizza into his mouth. It might have been his second, though.

Sofia eyed the open box of cheese pizza. Though her stomach rumbled, she worried about Snickers. Dr. Collins was still in the barn with Stephanie and Grace. Maybe she could offer to bring them some pizza and find out how Snickers was doing.

"I'll be right back, Grampy." Sofia reached for a handful of potato chips, crammed them into her mouth, and headed for the barn.

Snickers stood in the buckets of ice water while Grace stroked his neck. She waved when she noticed Sofia standing in the doorway.

Dr. Collins removed a paper from his clipboard and handed it to Stephanie. "Here are the instructions we talked about. Call me if you see him developing any signs of laminitis."

"Thank you," Stephanie said.

Sofia didn't want to hang around with this gruff, old man, but she thought it would be rude if she didn't offer him some pizza, especially since it was already seven o'clock. "We've got some pizza, if you want some, Dr. Collins."

"Oh, it's you." The vet stared at her, as if Sofia had suddenly appeared out of thin air or been magically transported into the barn. "Goodness no. I'm lactose intolerant."

Dr. Collins walked out the door. A moment later he reappeared. "But thank you for the offer, young lady." He turned and left again.

Grace smirked. "So, what do you think of our vet?"

Sofia looked at the floor and mumbled, "I don't know."

Stephanie touched Sofia's arm. "Dr. Collins is an excellent vet, but I'm afraid he's not really a people person. I want you to know that I'm very proud of you, Sofia."

"We're proud of all three of you," Grace added.

"But..." Sofia blinked back tears. "But it's our fault Snickers and Kit Kat escaped. None of this would have happened if we'd been more careful."

"It was an accident. Your Grampy told us what happened," Grace said. "You were feeling really sick, and I should have realized how serious it was. If anything, it's my fault. I should've sent you home right away when I saw that the heat was getting to you."

Sofia sniffed. *Don't cry. Don't cry.*

Stephanie's arms wrapped around Sofia, embracing her into a tight hug. Sofia stiffened. Then she melted against Stephanie's chest and began to sob.

"Is Snickers going to be alright?" Sofia gasped. She felt Stephanie's body convulse.

"I hope so."

It sounded like Stephanie was trying not to cry. Sofia remembered that Stephanie's horse, Toby, had died not that long ago. She had never asked what happened to him. She couldn't imagine how Stephanie would feel if she lost Snickers, too.

"What did Dr. Collins say?" Sofia asked between sniffs.

Stephanie gently released Sofia. "Well, he can't see any signs of laminitis at this point. But it's still early. We'll need to watch him carefully for a few days. Dr. Collins said the ice-water therapy is a good idea for the next forty-eight hours. We also need to soak his hay and give him some pain medicine and time to rest."

Sofia rubbed Snickers' forehead. "Standing in the ice-water won't give him frostbite, will it?"

"Dr. Collins said it won't hurt him, as long as he has a chance to rest and eat, too."

Olivia appeared at the entrance of the barn and gestured to Sofia. "If you don't get out here quick, Ryan's going to eat everything in sight."

"I'm starving," Grace said. "Maybe one of you can hold this pony while I get some pizza. I hope she bought veggie."

Sofia's stomach rumbled, but she took the lead rope.

"Don't be silly." Olivia snatched the lead from Sofia's fingers. "Go and eat."

A half-hour later, Sofia dumped the contents of a third bag of wood shavings into Snickers' stall. "Is this enough?"

"It needs to be really deep. I think you should add another one and fluff it up," said Stephanie. "Dr. Collins said it needs to be soft on his feet. We want him to be comfortable and lie down as much as possible in between soaking his feet. As soon as you're done we can put him in and give him a rest."

Sofia heard the clack, clack of Olivia's crutches as they hit the barn floor.

"Ryan wants to know how much longer to soak the hay," Olivia said.

"I'd give it a couple more minutes," Stephanie answered.

Sofia couldn't believe that hay could have much sugar in it, but the vet instructed them to soak Snickers' hay in water to rinse out any extra sugar. Snickers would have to eat the wet hay for at least two weeks.

"Okay, Snickerdoodles. Let's get you out of these buckets." Stephanie gently lifted the gelding's legs, and felt his hooves. "I bet you're ready for supper and some sleep."

"Here's the hay," Ryan said, leaving a puddle trailing behind him. He entered Snickers' stall and hung the drenched bag from a metal ring.

"Do you want to bring him in?" Stephanie offered the lead rope to Sofia.

Sofia led Snickers into the stall and removed his halter. The little gelding sniffed his hay bag and stared at her. *Poor thing.*

"Yes, that's your dinner." Sofia hugged Snickers' neck and gave him a kiss. "Go ahead. Eat it."

Snickers pulled a strand of hay from the net and began to chew. He didn't appear enthusiastic, but as there were no other options available, he reached for another bite.

Stephanie yawned. "Listen, kids. It's getting late. You've had a long day. I think it's time you went home."

"But what about Snickers?" Sofia pleaded. "I don't want to leave him."

"You're recovering from heat-stroke. You need as much rest as Snickers does. He'll be okay."

"But what about icing his feet?" Sofia asked.

Stephanie smiled. "I promise to ice his feet again after he's had some hay. Grace and I will check him throughout the night. The best thing you can do right now is to get some sleep. If you're feeling okay in the morning, you can come tomorrow."

"I want to help," Olivia said.

"Me too," added Ryan.

"Snickers is going to need lots of attention in the next few days. Let's work out a schedule with your families," Stephanie said. "We can take turns looking after Snickers."

Sofia reluctantly slid the stall door shut.

"So, Snickers will be okay in a couple of days, right?" Ryan asked.

"I hope so," said Stephanie. "He seems to be fine right now, but we can't see what's going on inside his body. We're going to need to check him 'round the clock for a couple of days."

"But we'll be able to take him to the Fourth of July parade, won't we?" Ryan asked.

Olivia pulled a frizzy wisp of hair from her eyes. "Please tell me you're just kidding."

"What? It's not for another five days." Ryan looked at Stephanie. "We've already got decorations and everything."

"I'm afraid Snickers is going to be on stall rest for at least a week," Stephanie said.

Ryan frowned. "What if we just took Kit Kat?"

A surge of anger pulsed through Sofia. "And leave Snickers behind?"

He shrugged. "It's just an idea."

How dare Ryan act like it didn't matter if they left Snickers behind?

Maybe he didn't know what it was like when people decided you were too much trouble to be bothered with. When you got in the way of other people's plans, and they decided to dump you off at your great-grandfather's house so they could spend the summer in England with their new boyfriend. When your father just disappeared one day and never saw you again for the rest of your life, because taking care of you just wasn't fun anymore. How would he feel, then?

"Well, it's a stupid idea," Olivia interjected. "Why don't we decorate the cart and dress you up as a horse. Then you can pull us."

Sofia imagined Olivia cracking a driving whip and shouting commands at Ryan, while she and Olivia rode in the cart and waved to the crowd. It would serve him right. Yes, she rather liked that idea.

Chapter 17

Sofia hopped in front of the closed barn door. She'd arrived ten minutes early for feeding time, too full of nervous energy to sit at her kitchen table staring at Grampy while he drank his coffee.

"Good morning, birthday girl," Stephanie called from across the driveway. "What does it feel like to be eleven?"

She remembered.

Sofia smiled and waved. "Good. How's Snickers?"

"Let's find out." Stephanie slid the door open.

Snickers whinnied and banged a hoof against the stall. Sofia worried that he would tear the barn down if he didn't go outside soon. She'd checked his hooves twice every day. No heat. No lameness.

Stephanie poured Snickers' vitamin supplement into his food bowl.

Sofia bent to pick it up. "It's been a week. Do you think he can go outside today?"

"We can check his feet after he finishes his breakfast. If there's still no sign of laminitis, you can lead him out to the paddock."

Sofia ran to Snickers' stall and slid open the door. "Here you go, buddy." The little gelding finished within seconds, as he always did.

"I'm going to check his feet now, okay?" Sofia usually filled the outside water bucket while the horses ate, but she didn't think she could wait another minute.

Stephanie laughed. "Go ahead."

Her pulse quickened as she ran her fingers down the sides of Snickers' left foreleg. Nothing. She examined his hoof for heat. It felt normal. She moved to his other side and repeated her actions. No signs of laminitis. She'd learned that laminitis usually affected only the front legs, but to be safe, she checked his hind legs.

"He's doing great."

"Can you lead him out to the aisle? I want to check him, too, and watch him move."

Stephanie examined Snickers and nodded to Sofia. "Snickerdoodles, you're good to go."

As Sofia led Snickers from the barn, he whinnied and danced at the end of his lead rope, full of restless energy. She opened the paddock gate, and closed it behind her before slipping off his halter. The tiny gelding leaped forward, kicking his hind legs into the air before galloping away.

When Stephanie led Kit Kat into the paddock, the mare joined Snickers' race around the enclosure. Sofia laughed as they whirled and bucked and squealed.

Then Snickers began to paw the dirt. He circled, bent his front knees and plopped onto the ground. He rolled onto his back, exposing his belly, kicking his legs into the air and snorting. After plastering both sides of his body with dust, Snickers got to his feet and shook himself like a dog. Sofia didn't think she had ever seen a happier horse.

***

Sofia sat at Grampy's kitchen table in front of the remains of an enormous chocolate cake and a half gallon container of melting ice cream. Ryan wiped his sleeve across his mouth. Olivia waved a bright blue envelope. Sofia had no idea what was inside that envelope, but whatever it was, it couldn't beat Snickers' gift that morning.

"Come on, open it!" Olivia demanded.

She tore open the envelope to reveal a handmade card. On the front was a palomino horse standing next to a girl with light brown skin and curly black hair.

"That's supposed to be you and Sundance," Ryan said. "I didn't have any pictures, so I hope I drew him right."

Sundance. One year ago today Gramma Lisa had given her the most beautiful horse in the world. Would she ever see him again? A lump formed in Sofia's throat.

She opened the card. *Happy birthday, Sofia!* was written in bubble letters.

"Thank you." Sofia closed the card. "It's a really nice drawing."

"Wait, there's more." Olivia handed her another envelope. "This goes with it."

Inside was a gift certificate to something called Funtown. "What's that?"

"Only the awesomest amusement park in Maine," Ryan said.

"Mom and Dad said they'll take us sometime soon." Olivia clapped her hands. "I hope you like roller coasters. Ryan's a total wimp and won't go with me."

Ryan rolled his eyes. "I *did* go on with you last summer."

"Yeah, once. But then you were too chicken to go again."

"It made my stomach hurt. I didn't want to puke."

Sofia had never been on a roller coaster. She thought she might prefer to stay safely on the ground with Ryan, but that wasn't something to worry about – yet.

"This one's from your mom." Grampy handed Sofia a present wrapped in pink paper, featuring cartoonish unicorns and rainbows.

I'm eleven years old, not six.

It felt like a large, hardcover book. She tore the paper.

"Pony Breeds of Great Britain," Sofia read.

"Wow, let me see." Olivia reached for the book and thumbed through the pages. "Ooh. An Exmoor pony. I read about those. Some of them still roam wild."

"There's a card that goes with it." Grampy passed Sofia a pink envelope.

Today's your birthday, the card proclaimed. Inside were two one-hundred dollar bills.

"Whoa. That's a lot of money," Ryan said.

Sofia didn't want to tell Ryan, but this gift didn't surprise her. She thought of the other birthdays and Christmases when Mom had left her with yet another relative or family friend. At first she had been excited to be given money, but she'd soon grown to resent it. How could her mother think money would make up for being absent from her life?

Olivia eyed the cash. "We should go to the mall for some school shopping. You won't have to do Goodwill now!"

"School?" Ryan groaned. "It's July."

"If she waits too long, all the good stuff will be sold out," Olivia said.

"No it won't," Ryan said.

Sofia's stomach lurched. The end of August would be here before she knew it. Where would she be going to school? If Mom had a plan, Sofia didn't know what it was. She didn't want to think about the summer ending.

There was one more gift on the table. She picked up the small package, wrapped in red and green plaid paper. She thought it looked more like Christmas paper than birthday paper, but she didn't mind, because she knew it must be from Grampy. She tore one corner of the wrapping.

"Is this...?" Sofia couldn't believe it. She ripped off the remaining paper.

Olivia shrieked. "A cell phone! You're so lucky."

"After all that mess at the barn last week, I thought it made sense. You know, for safety's sake," said Grampy. "I got one, too, so we can always get in touch with each other,"

"I can't believe you got me a phone." What would Mom say? Would she let her keep it? Maybe it would be better not to let her know.

"You'll have to show me how to use it, though." Grampy's mustache quivered. "The salesperson was going on and on about data, whatever that is. You only have a certain amount. You can't be on that thing constantly like I see all the kids doing these days."

Sofia smiled. "It's okay, Grampy. I promise not to get addicted or anything."

"Ryan and I are going to be the only kids in sixth grade without phones." Olivia sighed.

Sofia wished Olivia would stop talking about school.

***

Sofia paced in circles around her bedroom. Grampy was in the living room, watching the Red Sox lose to the Toronto Blue Jays, three to nothing. Olivia and Ryan had left an hour ago.

Having lived with Gramma Lisa for almost a year, Sofia wasn't about to forget her phone number. She hadn't heard from Gramma Lisa since the night when her mother had burst into the house, demanding that Sofia pack up her things. There'd been no calls or letters since then, not even an update about Sundance.

Sofia stared at her phone's screen. She'd already entered the familiar number into her contacts. All she had to do was hit the call icon next to Gramma Lisa's name.

Her finger hovered over the screen. Sofia took a deep breath and pressed the symbol.

The phone rang. Once. Twice. Three times.

"Hello?"

Sofia fought back tears at the sound of Gramma Lisa's familiar voice.

"It's Sofia."

There was a long pause.

"Hello?" Sofia asked. Maybe something had gone wrong with the call.

"Sofia... Does your mother know you're calling me?"

Sofia's pulse quickened. "Uh... No. She's in England."

Another pause.

"Yes, your Grampy told me she'd left."

He did? Grampy was in touch with Gramma Lisa? Why hadn't Grampy said anything about this?

"I love you, Sofia. You know that," Gramma Lisa's voice sounded more husky than usual.

"I love you, too."

"Your mom..." Gramma Lisa's voice trailed off.

What about Mom? What had she done to Gramma Lisa?

"She doesn't want me to have contact with you anymore."

"Why?" Sofia rubbed her stinging eyes.

"I'm sorry. I really... I messed up."

"I don't understand." It was Mom who messed up, not Gramma Lisa. Mom who'd dragged her away with no reason.

"Sundance misses you. But he's doing fine, and Deliah's fine, too. Someday maybe... hopefully soon..." her voice cracked.

"Please, Gramma Lisa – "

"I love you. Never forget that."

Then silence.

Sofia stared at her phone. *Call ended.*

Chapter 18

The morning breeze felt cool and pleasant on Sofia's arms and face as she leaned against the paddock fence. Leaves rustled overhead. An incessant chirp, chirp, chirp of an unseen bird rose over the trills and songs of his companions. Sofia breathed deeply, willing herself to forget the troubling questions swirling through her mind.

Stephanie emerged from the barn. "Nice job with the stalls. And the floor. It's cleaner in there than in my house." She rested her hand on Sofia's shoulder. "Would you like to take Snickers for a walk? We need to start exercising him again."

Sofia nodded.

"I'll tell Grace. I'm sure she'd like to join you."

"Okay." Sofia tried to smile. She should be excited to take Snickers on a walk, but it felt like a brick had settled into her stomach.

Stephanie cocked her head. "Hmm. Why don't you give Mr. Snickerdoodles a quick grooming while I let Grace know."

It was too beautiful a morning to groom Snickers inside the barn. After retrieving his halter, lead rope, and a box of brushes, Sofia tied the gelding to a fence post in his paddock. She checked his feet first. No heat. She picked up each one and removed the packed dirt and dried manure from his hooves.

"Hey there," called Grace. "Can Kit Kat and I come for a walk with you?"

Grace led her chestnut mare out of the paddock and down the driveway. Sofia and Snickers followed. Instead of turning left towards Grampy's house, Grace crossed the road and went right, skirting the edge of a recently-hayed field. Large round bales were haphazardly grouped beside an old tractor.

They turned up a dirt path along the far side of the field, disturbing a family of wild turkeys. Snickers stopped abruptly, raised his head, and snorted. Sofia stroked his neck, and the pinto relaxed.

"You're awfully quiet," Grace remarked. "Is something wrong? Or are you just enjoying this lovely morning?"

Sofia hesitated. "I'm okay," she mumbled.

"You don't sound so sure."

Grace pointed to a gap between two large pine trees. "There's a nice little trail through the woods. Wanna see?"

"Okay." Sofia hoped Grace wouldn't ask her questions about how she was feeling. The truth was, she didn't really know. For months she'd wondered why Gramma Lisa never tried to call her or even send her a letter or pictures of Sundance. Now she knew it was her mother's fault. It was so unfair of Mom to force them apart like that, even if Gramma Lisa had messed up somehow. And if Grampy had been in touch with Gramma Lisa, why hadn't he said anything to her about it?

They turned into the woods. Dried leaves and pine needles crunched beneath the horses' feet, releasing a damp, earthy smell as they began to climb a gentle slope. The trees grew more closely together here and the dappled sunlight faded into deep shade.

"You seem so sad today. Are you missing your mother?" Grace asked.

"No. I mean, I don't know..." Sofia's throat burned. This wasn't the right way to answer Grace's question. More questions would be sure to follow now.

Grace halted and turned to face Sofia and Snickers. "It sounds like it's kind of complicated."

"Yeah." Sofia didn't meet Grace's gaze.

"It's like that with my father," Grace said, turning back to lead Kit Kat over a fallen branch.

Snickers stopped and sniffed the branch before stepping over it.

"Dad left us when I was about your age," said Grace. "He and Mom fought a lot. I used to think I could stop it from happening by trying to get them to listen to each other. But they usually just got mad at me and told me to mind my own business. Especially Dad."

Sofia brushed a deerfly from Snickers' white ear. She hoped Grace wouldn't ask about her father.

"When my dad got a new girlfriend with her own kids, he stopped visiting us. I thought it was my fault. But it wasn't my fault. It took me a long time to understand that."

The path veered sharply to the right. Grace turned her head towards Sofia, who looked away, pretending not to notice.

"You know it isn't your fault, Sofia. Parents make their own decisions. And sometimes those decisions hurt."

Sofia blinked back tears. *I know.*

***

As Sofia and Snickers followed Grace and Kit Kat down the driveway, she noticed the Murphy's white van parked beside the barn. Pastor Amy pulled Olivia's wheelchair out of the back.

"Come on, Mom. I'm not going to use that stupid thing," Olivia grumbled.

"You don't have to use it," Pastor Amy said.

"Then why do you always leave it here?"

"Just in case you need it." Pastor Amy pushed the wheelchair in the direction of the picnic table.

Ryan bounded toward Grace and Kit Kat, making kissing noises. "How's my little sweetie horse?"

Olivia shook her head and covered her eyes. "I don't know how we could possibly be related."

Ten minutes later, Grace called the Mini Whinnies meeting to order. "Snickers is doing great, so we can start gentle exercise with him. Sofia took him on a walk this morning. Hopefully he'll be ready to start pulling the cart again, soon, since Olivia's been doing such a great job with that."

Sofia felt a twinge of jealousy. Grace let her drive Snickers some-times, but most of the time she and Ryan had to take turns working with Kit Kat.

"So for today, we're going to practice jumping with Kit Kat." Grace nodded at Sofia. "Sofia's our expert, so I'm going to ask her to tell us about the kinds of jumping classes at miniature horse shows."

"So we're going?" Ryan asked.

"We'll see. Right now we're just learning, okay?"

Olivia scowled.

Oh, no. What's wrong with her today?

"Sofia, if Ryan goes to a horse show with Kit Kat, what are two types of jumping classes that he might enter?" prompted Grace.

"Hunter and jumper." Sofia hadn't expected Grace to ask her to give a report on this subject.

Grace nodded. "What's the difference between hunter and jumper?"

Sofia closed her eyes in concentration. "In hunter, the judge cares about how the horse looks. They judge the horse's manners and their form while going through the jumping course. You're supposed to keep an even pace. You're not supposed to slow down and speed up."

"Great answer," Grace said. "I couldn't have given it better myself. And how is jumper different?"

This was easy. "It doesn't matter what you look like. It's all about points."

"You mean faults, not points," Olivia corrected her.

Sofia felt her cheeks grow hot. "Oh, yeah."

"I don't get it," said Ryan.

Grace bolted from the picnic table, startling Sofia. "Hey, I have an idea. Let's set up a jump. Olivia can be our judge and tell us about our faults."

"Yeah, she's good at that," muttered Ryan.

"That's because you have about a billion of them," Olivia grumbled.

The Mini Whinnies entered the horses' dirt paddock, which doubled as a practice area. Ryan and Sofia moved a set of wooden jumping standards and poles to the center. Snickers appeared disinterested, continuing to munch on his hay, but Kit Kat followed them to the jump, which they set at two feet high.

"Okay, Olivia, you're the judge. And Ryan, Sofia, and I are horses." Grace began to prance like a nervous racehorse. She pretended to canter up to the jump, but instead of jumping over it, she stopped in front of it and whinnied.

Sofia and Ryan laughed.

"So, Judge Olivia, how many faults is that?"

"Four." Olivia sighed dramatically.

"So if your horse refuses the jump, you get four faults. If it happens again, you get four more faults. And if it happens a third time, you're disqualified. If the horse stops in front but then pops over at the last second, you don't get any faults. If that happened in hunter, it would be bad. But it doesn't matter in jumper. All that matters is that your horse clears the jump."

Ryan snorted and whinnied. "My turn!" He ran up to the jump and crashed through it.

Sofia held her sides as she convulsed with laughter. "That's what Snickers would do."

Olivia rolled her eyes. "Four faults."

"Right again, Judge Olivia. But what about this?" Grace trotted towards the jump, but instead of leaping over it, she made a big circle, returned to the obstacle, and jumped over.

Olivia scratched her neck. "So that's not a refusal?"

"Nope. It's circling. That might happen if your horse is going too fast for you and you need to slow it down. Sofia, how many faults for circling?"

"Three faults." Sofia knew something that Olivia didn't. She smiled, but didn't dare look her friend in the eye.

"So how do you win the jumper class?" Ryan asked.

Her confidence buoyed, Sofia gave the answer. "The one with the fewest faults wins. If there's a tie, they put the jumps up higher and the horses that are tied for first place run the course again. And depending on the rules of the show, they either keep making the jumps higher and higher until the tie is broken, or they turn it into a timed course. If they have the same score, the fastest horse wins."

"You got it, girl!" Grace gave Sofia a high-five. "And please excuse my bragging, but Kit Kat and I were youth jumper champions for three years in a row. She may be tiny, but in her day we could beat every horse out there."

Grace gave Kit Kat a pat. "It's been a few years, but now a new generation of Mini Whinnies is rising up to reclaim the championship. Who is it going to be? Sofia? Ryan? Olivia?"

"Olivia? Yeah, right." Olivia's voice felt like icicles stabbing Sofia's heart. "What's your problem, Grace?"

Sofia's eyes widened. Didn't Grace realize it would be impossible for Olivia to run around a jump course with Kit Kat?

"Do you think this is funny?" Olivia slammed one of her crutches to the ground. "Well, I don't.

Neither did Sofia.

Chapter 19

Sofia stared, open mouthed, as Olivia pounded the dirt with her remaining crutch. Her friend's reddened face nearly matched the color of her fiery hair. Sofia had never seen Olivia this furious.

"I quit," she spat. "Who needs this stupid club!"

"Now there's my firecracker." Grace's voice sounded remarkably calm, but her stern expression unnerved Sofia. Moments ago, Grace's playful exuberance reminded Sofia of a little kid, but now Grace resembled a younger version of Stephanie.

"Shut up! I'm not your firecracker." Olivia bent to retrieve her other crutch. "I want to go home."

Ryan cowered behind Sofia.

Sofia's heart pounded. How could Grace be so insensitive? She wanted to stand up for Olivia, but what should she say?

"Come on, Olivia," Grace said, hands on her hips. "You're a fighter, not a quitter."

Olivia straightened and narrowed her eyes.

Grace didn't flinch under Olivia's glare. "I remember the first day I met you. You were seven years old. It was one of my first times volunteering at the therapeutic riding center. I saw your father helping you out of your wheelchair, and Miss Jessica told me it was your first time back after having surgery. You were so tiny and Molly was so enormous. I was terrified you'd get hurt."

Sofia remembered Olivia's obvious pride in the model horse that had been painted to look like Molly, and her flash of anger when Sofia expressed surprise that she could ride.

"I knew you were in pain, and probably a lot of it. But nothing would stop you from getting on that horse. Nothing. Every time I saw you at the barn, it felt like you were daring the world to try and stop you. What I want to know, is what's stopping you now?"

Sofia held her breath.

Olivia's shoulders slumped and she dropped her head. "I can't do it."

"Why not?"

Sofia felt like she might explode. *Because she can't run, Grace. Why are you torturing her?*

"Look at me," Olivia snapped. "In case you haven't noticed, I have a hard enough time just walking."

Grace pointed toward the barn. "Every time your mother drops you off, she leaves your wheelchair. And every time we meet, you pretend it doesn't exist."

"I hate that stupid thing," Olivia grumbled.

"Well, if you stopped being so darn stubborn you might figure out that there are times when that stupid thing could actually help you. Instead of moping around and getting mad at your brother for doing the things you think you can't do, you could actually participate."

"I don't do that."

Grace cocked her head and raised an eyebrow.

"Whatever." Olivia frowned and glanced in the direction of her wheelchair. "You really think I could lead Kit Kat over the jumps?"

"I don't see why not."

But wouldn't that scare the horses? Sofia didn't dare to ask. She tried to imagine how Snickers might react. He'd probably stare at it and snort like it was some kind of monster. But he was a smart horse. He might get used to it if they practiced enough. Kit Kat had a gentler disposition. Maybe it wouldn't be a problem for her at all.

"I don't know how well I can hold the lead rope while pushing myself over this kind of ground," Olivia said.

"I could push you," Sofia volunteered.

"Or I could," offered Ryan.

"Sounds like an awesome plan to me," Grace said. "Want to give it a try?"

Olivia nodded. "As long as Sofia does it. I don't want my brother pushing me around."

***

Sofia stood behind Olivia, her fingers clenched around the handles of her friend's wheelchair. A bead of sweat dripped down her back.

Grace stroked Kit Kat's neck. The mare didn't appear frightened. She reached her neck forward towards Olivia's outstretched hand. Moments later, Kit Kat's nose nuzzled Olivia's lap.

So far, so good.

Grace passed the lead rope to Ryan. "Could you lead Kit Kat beside your sister while Sofia pushes her? I want Kit Kat to get used to having the wheelchair beside her."

Sofia had never pushed a wheelchair, and worried that if she went too fast Olivia might lose her balance and tumble out. She inched along, with Ryan and Kit Kat stepping beside them.

"I think if this were a jump-off, we might break the world record," Olivia said, "for the slowest time ever recorded."

Grace laughed. "Kit Kat seems to be handling this well. Sofia, I think you can pick up the pace a bit."

Sofia dropped her eyes to avoid Ryan's smirk. She gripped the handles tightly and walked forward at a normal pace. Olivia didn't fall out.

"Great. Let's try a trot," Grace suggested.

Ryan clucked, and Kit Kat lurched forward.

Sofia had to push harder for a few steps, but once they gained momentum it wasn't difficult to keep up with Kit Kat's stride.

"Are you ready?" Grace asked Olivia.

"I was born ready," sang Olivia. "Don't care if the world ain't ready for me."

"Alrighty, then." Grace chuckled. "You three can take a break for a minute."

She better not fall out. Sofia pulled Olivia's wheelchair to a stop without incident.

"Now Sofia, this is going to take some practice. You might feel like you're responsible for Kit Kat because you're pushing Olivia. But Olivia is the one leading Kit Kat, so she's the one in charge. You need to pay attention to what Olivia tells you to do."

Ryan playfully punched Sofia on the arm. "Now you'll know how I feel."

Sofia grinned. "Olivia's the boss."

"And don't you forget it," Olivia said.

"Okay, sis, here's your horse." Ryan passed Kit Kat's lead to Olivia, and stepped aside. Even in the wheelchair, Olivia's shoulders were several inches above Kit Kat's withers.

Sofia stood with her hands on the wheelchair's grips. She couldn't see Olivia's face. "How will I know what you want me to do?"

Grace brushed a purple streak of hair from her eyes. "I think you should keep it simple. Maybe just start out with commands like walk, trot, halt, and that sort of thing. Olivia can tell you faster or slower."

"And what about turning?" Sofia asked. If they were going to navigate a jump course, they wouldn't be going straight all the time.

"I know," Olivia said, "I'll tell you gee and haw."

"What the heck does that mean?" Ryan asked.

Sofia was glad he asked first. The words sounded like nonsense to her, and she didn't want Olivia to think she was stupid.

Olivia wiggled her head and shoulders as if she were dancing in her wheelchair. "That's what farmers sometimes say to steer their draft horses. Gee is right and haw is left."

That's totally confusing. Sofia had a hard enough time remembering which way was right and left. And pushing a wheelchair made it impossible for her to make the L-shaped hand clue she had been taught in first grade.

"I think left and right might work better," Grace said. "We don't want it to be too complicated."

Olivia shrugged. "I thought it sounded cool, but whatever. Okay, Sofia, walk."

Sofia pushed. Olivia guided Kit Kat. And together, they walked forward. They turned left. They halted. They walked forward again. The right-hand turn presented more challenges, as they had to push the wheelchair in the direction towards Kit Kat, but the little mare appeared unconcerned.

"Trot," Olivia commanded.

Sofia's stomach fluttered, but she followed Olivia's directions. Kit Kat trotted obediently, her nose even with Olivia's hand.

"Faster."

Sofia ran faster, breathing hard.

Kit Kat broke into a canter. Olivia whooped. Her hair streamed behind her, tickling Sofia's hands.

Grace cheered. "Awesome! But don't kill Sofia."

"Okay." Olivia laughed. "Slower."

"Thanks," said Sofia. Running while pushing a wheelchair over the dirt was a lot harder than she had expected, but she couldn't stop smiling. She was proud of Kit Kat, and proud of Olivia. Covering a jump course would be challenging, but she felt confident that they could master it with practice.

"Are you ready to try that jump?" asked Grace.

"Absolutely," Olivia shouted.

"You've seen Sofia do it many times," Grace said. "Remember to lift your arm as Kit Kat jumps so the lead rope doesn't tangle up with the jump. Give her some room."

The first time Sofia had attempted to lead Snickers over a jump, she didn't raise her arm high enough. The wooden jumping standard holding the pole in place crashed under her feet, and the pole flew sideways into Snickers' hind legs. It would be a disaster if this happened with Olivia in the wheelchair. She couldn't think about that now.

They trotted along the far side of the paddock. The jump had been placed in the center and set at twelve inches. It would be an easy hop for Kit Kat as long as they approached it at the right angle. Sofia took a deep breath to steady her nerves.

"Left," Olivia directed. "Now straight."

They were on track, with Kit Kat heading right for the center of the jump. Olivia needed to be close to the jump, but if Sofia pushed her too close, the wheelchair might knock into it.

They were three strides away. Sofia looked from the jumping standard to wheel. It was going to be close.

Two strides away.

One.

Sofia held her breath.

Kit Kat's front legs left the ground, and Olivia lifted the lead rope above her head. The mare tucked her front legs to her chest, her powerful hind legs thrusting her higher and forward over the jump.

For a fraction of a second, all four of her feet floated above the pole. Then Kit Kat's front legs stretched forward and reached for the ground. Her hind legs cleared the jump and the mare landed, continuing forward in a steady trot. Sofia pushed Olivia, keeping pace with the horse.

Ryan jumped up and down. "You did it!"

"Walk," Olivia said.

Sofia's arms felt wobbly and her calf muscles burned.

"Halt."

"I knew you could do it." Grace gave Olivia a high-five.

"Can you take her for a minute?" Olivia gave Kit Kat to Grace. She turned her wheelchair around to face Sofia.

"Thank you so much," she said, hugging Sofia. "We make a good team, don't we?"

Sofia felt tears sting her eyes, and blinked them away. "Yes, we do."

Chapter 20

The bumper cars weren't Sofia's favorite ride at Funtown. Antique cars were more her thing. No unexpected crashes. No whiplash. And the metal track made it so you didn't have to know how to steer particularly well.

Sofia's neck whipped sideways as her vehicle bounced against the car next to her.

"Ha! Got you, again," shouted Ryan.

A moment later, Olivia laughed as she collided head on into Sofia.

Mercifully, the bumper cars slowed, then stopped. Sofia rubbed the back of her neck and she untangled herself from the vehicle's restraints.

The ride attendant ushered them toward the exit where Olivia had parked her wheelchair. It remained unoccupied most of the time, unless they had to walk a distance to the next ride. Sofia observed that as much as Olivia hated using it, bringing the wheelchair had one advantage. They didn't have to wait in any lines. They were allowed to enter most of the rides through the exit.

Sofia pushed the empty wheelchair as they left the bumper car ride.

"Oh," Ryan exclaimed, pointing to the brightly lit carousel in front of them. "We have to ride the horses."

"You're such a baby," Olivia teased. "I'm embarrassed to know you."

"Aw, come on." Ryan threw a fake punch at his sister. "You're always on my case about being scared to ride horses. Now that I want to ride one you call me a baby."

Sofia laughed. "You should try that big black one with the wild looking mane. That is, if you dare."

"Nah. I have my eye on the white one with the roses on her saddle." He winked at Sofia.

Olivia hit her forehead with the palm of her hand and groaned.

"I'll take the palomino one, in honor of Sundance." Sofia turned to Olivia. "Please go on with us. After all, I'm here to celebrate my birthday."

"Oh, alright. I'll do it for you," Olivia said. "But I'll have to pick one of the small ones that are supposed to be for the little kids." She tapped her leg. "Kind of hard to get on the big ones, you know. And there's no way I'm sitting on the bench thing like some old person."

Sofia's stomach sank. *I'm so stupid.* Olivia had experienced only minor challenges getting into the bumper cars, the log flume, and the Tilt-a Whirl. But the merry-go-round? Sofia hadn't thought about how difficult it would be for Olivia to mount a wobbling carousel horse without someone lifting her. She and Ryan could help her, but that might embarrass Olivia. She considered backing out, and telling Ryan he'd have to ride alone. But she wondered if that might make her friend feel even more awkward.

The line for the carousel was short, consisting of a handful of cranky and over-excited young children and their exhausted parents. They had their pick of the horses. Sofia walked beside Olivia, waiting for her to choose her mount.

"This poor thing is as small as Snickers." Olivia stood next to the left side of the horse, which Sofia knew was the correct side for an equestrian to mount even when your horse was made out of plastic. "Can you stand next to me while I get on?"

Sofia nodded, surprised that Olivia asked for help.

"Thanks." Olivia handed her crutches to Sofia. "This is kind of tricky, but I can get my leg over." Olivia gripped the carousel horse's pole with both hands and eased into the saddle.

Ryan scrambled onto a much bigger horse in the same row. The horse's head arched high, black mane spilling over its neck, its mouth open and teeth showing. Like most of the others, its body was white, but Sofia didn't see any roses.

"Hey, Ryan, wanna race?" Olivia asked. She was now astride her mount.

Sofia approached the cream-colored horse sandwiched between her friends. She smiled as she grabbed the golden pole and swung her leg over her steed's back. When was the last time she'd ridden on a carousel?

The tinny organ music stirred a long forgotten memory. *"Mija."* Her father wrapped his muscular arm protectively around her waist. Her mother stroked her hair. She couldn't have been older than three.

Sofia's horse moved forward, rising a few inches before gliding back down.

Olivia flashed a smile as her horse rose into the air.

"Look, no hands." Ryan's outstretched arm brushed Sofia's horse as it headed back up.

"Show off." Olivia grinned. "But you know my horse is the fastest. We're going to win this race."

"We'll see about that," he replied.

Sofia leaned forward in the saddle and closed her eyes. "Come on, boy, you can do it." She remembered the nervous thrill of galloping on Sundance, his powerful muscles rippling beneath her, the wind tossing her hair.

As the ride slowed, Ryan declared his horse the winner. Olivia insisted that it was a three-way tie. The twins continued to tease each other about the outcome of the race as they exited the carousel.

"Sofia should be the winner, since she's the birthday—" Ryan was interrupted by a taunting voice.

"Aww, wook at widdle Wyan widing the widdle horsies."

Sofia snapped her head to the right, trying to locate the source of the insult. It belonged to a tall boy with longish blond hair. He looked to be about their age or a little older.

Ryan ducked and hunched his shoulders, as if trying to disappear.

The boy waved at Ryan and made a whinnying sound. His two companions guffawed.

"Shut up, James," Olivia growled.

"Wanna make me?" James hissed, stepping forward. "I'd love to see you try."

A shorter boy on James' left pointed at Olivia, smirking. "Watch out for her. She'll whack you over the head with her crutches."

The girl beside him cackled.

Olivia's face flushed and her body grew rigid.

Sofia felt the heat rise in her cheeks, too. The girl's ridiculing laughter reminded her of Anna Jordan, a bully from her school in Connecticut. She'd spent half of fifth grade doing her best to avoid Anna, who delighted in making a show of sniffing the air and claiming that Sofia stank like a horse. Not one of her classmates came to her defense.

"Leave them alone." The words sprang from Sofia's mouth before she knew they were forming there. She swallowed. *What have I done?*

James narrowed his eyes at Sofia. Then he grinned. "I don't believe it. Ryan's got a girlfriend." He made a kissing noise.

His companions howled.

"She's not his girlfriend!" Olivia shouted.

"Aw, wooks wike widdle Wyan's sister's jealwous," taunted James.

Sofia's eyes darted from Olivia to Ryan and back to Olivia again. *It's time to get out of here.*

The mean girl tossed her long brown hair and put an arm around James' shoulders, a triumphant look plastered across her face. "That's not Ryan's girlfriend... she must be Olivia's."

The bullies laughed raucously as the brown-haired girl sang, "Olivia's got a girlfriend, Olivia's got a girlfriend."

Sofia's face burned. Her hands shook. She refused to look at this nasty girl or her companions. "Let's get some fried dough," she muttered through clenched teeth, though she thought she might throw up if she tried to eat some.

Ryan remained frozen in place.

"Come on," Olivia hissed in his ear.

James and his companions snickered as they turned and walked away. The girl moved oddly, hunched over and shuffling along.

As Sofia realized that the girl was trying to imitate Olivia, her humiliation flared into rage. She wanted to hurl herself at the girl, to grab her hair, to slap her face. Fist balled, she lurched forward.

"No," Olivia warned.

Sofia opened her mouth, and snapped it shut. Whatever she said would only make the situation worse. She waited until the bullies were out of earshot before she allowed her shaking voice to spit out the question. "Who are those jerks?"

Ryan looked pale. "Just some kids from my class. I don't really want to talk about it." He lowered himself onto an empty bench.

Olivia sat next to him and put her hand over his. "Don't let them get to you."

Sofia stood awkwardly beside the twins, unsure of whether to sit or remain standing.

Olivia looked up, face still flushed. "So, do you want to get some fried dough? 'Cause I'm starving."

***

Sofia yawned and turned onto her side. The fabric of her sleeping bag rustled against the carpeted floor in Olivia's bedroom. The glowing numbers of the clock on the desk changed from 12:22 to 12:23. Maybe she'd drunk too much soda while watching a movie in the Murphy's living room. She wished she could just get comfortable and fall asleep.

Where will I live after the summer's over?

For weeks she'd stubbornly refused to consider what might happen if Mom didn't permit her return to Gramma Lisa's house for the start of school. Sure, Mom could hold a grudge, but she must realize how wrong it would be to separate Sofia from her own family, and from Sundance. But Gramma Lisa wasn't even allowed to talk with Sofia on the phone. Mom had never done that before.

Her stomach knotted as she imagined having to move again.

Sofia had to find a way to convince Mom to make up with Gramma Lisa. Whatever Mom's disagreement was, the whole thing was dreadfully unfair. She rubbed her eyes and sighed.

"Are you still awake?" Olivia whispered.

"Yeah," Sofia mumbled into her pillow.

"I thought so," Olivia said. "I've been thinking about what happened today. You know with James and Emily and that kid, Lucas."

"Uh..." Sofia flipped onto her back. Olivia must be talking about the bullies at the amusement park. "The mean kids?"

"Yes, them." Sofia could hear her friend shifting restlessly under her sheets. After a long pause Olivia added, "Thanks for sticking up for us."

"No problem. That's what friends do." Sofia wished she had a friend who would stand up to Mom and tell her how wrong it was to take her away from Gramma Lisa and Sundance.

"I've never had a friend like you before," Olivia said so quietly that Sofia had to strain to hear her.

"What do you mean?" Sofia wondered what would make her different from any of Olivia's other friends. Maybe because they shared a love of horses?

Olivia didn't say anything for such a long time that Sofia wondered if she'd fallen asleep.

"You treat me like a normal person, I guess," Olivia said. "Most kids act all weird around me."

"Like those bullies at Funtown?" It must be horrible to have people make fun of the way you walk.

"Sometimes. But most kids aren't mean to me that way. The problem is everyone basically ignores me. Like they know they shouldn't make fun of me because that would be rude, but they don't want to be friends with me, either. They might say 'hi,, but they don't include me in anything. It's like I'm not even a real person to them."

Olivia adjusted her pillow. "So in a way, those kids are worse than bullies. At least with people like James and Emily I know where I stand, and I can try to avoid them. But it's hard to ignore the fact that every kid in school acts like I'm invisible."

Sofia couldn't imagine an invisible Olivia. Her dramatic personality was hard to ignore. "But you're such an amazing person. You can sing and play guitar and ride horses. And you're so smart, and not just about horses. I bet you're one of the best students in your school."

"Thanks," Olivia said. "See, you're a true friend because you know all that stuff about me. And of course, you're right. I'm the best student in my class. I've never gotten anything less than an A my entire life."

Sofia smiled as she imagined Olivia bragging to her classmates about her report card or pointing out when they'd gotten a math problem wrong.

"But, no one cares about that stuff. All they see is a kid who can't walk the way they do. I guess it makes them feel uncomfortable." Olivia's voice hardened. "Do you know you're the first friend who has ever come to my house for a sleepover?"

"No," Sofia said. She'd never considered the possibility that Olivia might need a friend just as much as she did. "Thanks for inviting me."

Olivia sighed. "I wish you didn't have to leave at the end of the summer."

Sofia pulled a corner of the sleeping bag over her cheek. "Neither do I," she whispered.

Was that true? *Do I really want to stay?*

"I thought you wanted to go back to live with your Gramma. And Sundance."

Sofia swallowed back the lump in her throat. If Mom refused to let her return to Gramma Lisa's, would Grampy allow her to live at his house and attend school with Olivia and Ryan? She could continue to help Grace and Stephanie take care of Snickers and Kit Kat.

But what about Sundance? A tear trickled down her cheek.

Sofia sniffed. "Something bad happened between Mom and Gramma Lisa. I'm afraid she might not let me live there anymore."

"Oh," Olivia said. "I thought that might be a problem."

Sofia sat up. "What do you mean?"

"Well..."

Sofia's throat tightened. "Well, what?"

"I kind of overheard your Grampy and my mom talking once after church. It was before I met you."

"What did you hear?" Sofia demanded.

Olivia paused.

"What did you hear?" Sofia's voice sounded harsher than she intended. Grampy must be keeping a secret from her. He had told Pastor Amy about it. Did he tell other people? Did everyone at church know all about her private business?

"That your mother thought it wasn't safe for you to live there anymore."

"What are you talking about?" Sofia's face grew hot.

"I thought you knew," Olivia's voice wavered. "I figured you didn't bring it up because you didn't want to talk about it."

"Tell me what Grampy said." How could all these people, people she loved and cared about, talk about her behind her back? *I deserve to know why Mom is keeping me from Gramma Lisa and Sundance.*

"I don't know." Olivia hesitated. "I didn't hear any details. I guess I assumed you were being abused or something."

"Gramma Lisa never abused me!" Sofia slammed her fist into the floor. How could Mom possibly think that?

"Hey, don't yell at me. I'm just telling you what I thought they were talking about."

"Sorry." Sofia knew it wasn't Olivia's fault.

"Maybe I got it wrong."

"It's my mother who's got it wrong," fumed Sofia. "I don't know why she thinks that I'm not safe there, but she's wrong."

"You should tell her, then," Olivia said.

"Yeah, I will."

Once Mom got an idea stuck in her mind, she didn't let go easily. That was, until her next great idea pushed the old one aside. Could Sofia find a way to bring Mom and Gramma Lisa back together? *I have to convince her.*

Chapter 21

Sofia sat across the picnic table from Ryan and Olivia, awaiting the start of their miniature horse club meeting. She stifled a yawn. Despite turning it over and over in her mind for most of the night, she couldn't imagine what she could say to convince Mom to make up with Gramma Lisa.

"What are we doing today?" Ryan asked.

Grace tilted her head and made a face like a teacher about to scold a classroom of naughty children. "Patience, young man. You know the drill by now."

Sofia covered her mouth to hide her grin. According to her phone, it was 7:59. Mini Whinnies met at exactly eight in the morning. Grace had always refused to begin even a minute early. Even though they were the only three kids in the club, Grace loved to act as if it were a formal affair. It reminded Sofia of the way the grown-ups ran the summer business meeting at the Good Shepherd Community Church, only a lot less boring.

Grace wound her fingers through her hair before checking her phone. "I call this meeting of the Mini Whinnies to order."

"Finally," muttered Ryan.

"Do I need to assign you extra mucking duty?"

He ducked his head. "Oh, no. I'm good, thanks."

Grace clutched her clipboard to her chest. "One of the club's goals was to compete at a horse show. Are you still up for the challenge?"

Sofia's hand shot into the air. "I am!"

"Me, too," Ryan added.

Olivia wiggled in her seat and shifted her shoulders from side to side. "Will there be a jumping class?"

Grace nodded and held the clipboard above her head. "I've got the show's class list right here. We only have two horses, and you're all in

125

the eight to twelve-year-old division, so you'll have to decide how to divide up the classes. But each of you will be able to enter a few."

"Snickers is no good at jumping," Olivia said. "But Kit Kat is awesome."

Sofia's stomach tightened. She and Olivia were a team. But Sofia really wanted to be the one leading Kit Kat over the jumps. She'd been practicing most of the summer while Olivia got to drive Snickers. What if Olivia wanted to drive and do the jumping class? She pushed back a pang of jealousy. Hopefully the show offered more than one kind of jumping event.

Grace removed a paper from the clipboard and placed it on the table in front of Sofia. "This is the class list."

Ryan scooted from his seat, raced to Sofia's side of the table, and peered over her shoulder.

Sofia scanned the paper. There were classes for showmanship, halter, costume, obstacle, and driving. True, Snickers didn't jump well, but unlike Kit Kat, he could pull a cart. There were two classes for driving in her age group; youth driving and driving obstacles. And, yes! There were separate hunter and jumper classes. Maybe she and Olivia could compromise.

"Let me see it, too." Olivia reached across the picnic table and snatched the sheet.

"I'm not done yet," protested Ryan.

Grace cleared her throat and took the paper from Olivia. "Let's go over this together. We've worked on most of the skills needed for these classes, but you might not understand what you need to do in each specific one."

She pointed to the first item on the list. "Showmanship is almost always the first event at a horse show. Do any of you know why?"

Sofia looked at Olivia, who shrugged. Ryan shook his head.

"If you want to do well in showmanship, you and your horse need to be clean and neat. And believe me, it's hard to stay clean and neat all day when you're at a show," Grace said. "In the showmanship class, the goal is to show the judge how amazing your horse looks and how well your horse responds to you. The judge will inspect both of you and you'll be asked to lead your horse through a simple pattern. You'll need to groom your horse to perfection, and you need to look your best, too."

Sofia thought it would make her nervous to have to look perfect in front of a judge. "Did you ever win showmanship?"

Grace laughed. "It wasn't my thing, really. My brother, Kevin, was better at it than I was. He always stood up straight and smiled at the judge. He and Snickers won a lot."

"Do you think I could win with Kit Kat?" Ryan sat straighter and smiled.

"I don't see why not. Do you own a suit?"

"Yeah, my parents made me dress up for Easter."

"Good. You could wear it, and boots and a cowboy hat and gloves. Maybe you can borrow some of Kevin's old stuff."

"What about all those halter classes?" Olivia asked. "They have so many different categories. They take up half the show. What's that about?"

Grace brushed a strand of purple hair from her eyes. "Miniature horse shows always have lots of halter classes. In showmanship, the handler is the one who is judged on how they present themselves and their horse. But in halter, it's only the horse that's judged. The winner is supposed to be the horse that best fits the ideal standard of the breed. Halter is so popular that they often divide the classes up into categories according to the horses' ages, colors, and gender."

"Is it kind of like a beauty pageant for horses?" Sofia imagined that Snickers would win a class like that with his gorgeous blue eyes.

"Like Miss America for miniature horses?" Grace smiled. "I never thought of it in that way, but I suppose so."

"What halter class would Snickers be in?" Sofia asked.

Grace studied the paper for a moment. "In your age group, it would be multicolor geldings. That's for horses that have either pinto or appaloosa coat colors."

"I want to do that class." With Snickers' unusual pinto markings, he'd win a blue ribbon to match his eyes.

Grace nodded. "Most of the winning horses in halter are younger than Snickers, but I bet you would do a fantastic job with him." She tapped her clipboard. "So after all the halter classes finish there's a lunch break. Then there's the costume class, which is super fun. Like dressing up for Halloween."

"You told us about that one before," said Ryan. "And I have an idea. I want to dress Kit Kat up like a giant, furry spider. I'll have to find a way to attach four extra legs to her. That would be so cool!"

Grace's eyes widened. "A giant spider. That's definitely Halloween-ish."

Sofia shuddered. She didn't like spiders one bit.

"But what about you?" Olivia asked her twin. "You have to dress up, too. Something to go with a spider."

Ryan shrugged. "I don't know. Maybe Spiderman?"

"That's lame." Olivia smirked. "I think you should be Little Miss Muffet. 'Cause you get scared all the time."

Oh no. They're going to fight.

But instead of arguing, Ryan burst out laughing.

Olivia recited the nursery rhyme with a sing-song voice. "Little Miss Muffet sat on her tuffet, eating her curds and whey. When along came a spider and sat down beside her and frightened Miss Muffet away."

"I am so going to win that class," Ryan gasped between guffaws.

Sofia giggled. "You're going to dress up like a girl?"

"Why not?" Ryan curtseyed.

Olivia shook her head. "I don't know you." But she was grinning.

"That's certainly original," Grace said. "I've been to quite a few horse shows, and I can honestly say I've never seen a Miss Muffet and spider costume. Usually the cute little kids win, but I think it would be hard for a judge not to give you a ribbon for something like that."

Ryan pouted. "What? Are you saying I'm not cute?"

Olivia rolled her eyes.

Grace continued to review the list of classes. Sofia and Ryan agreed that they didn't mind competing against each other in halter obstacle, a class where they would lead their horses through a series of obstacles and movements. There would be a time limit to complete each one correctly. To place well, they would need to memorize the course and navigate each area according to the specific directions given by the judge. Ryan wanted to enter with Kit Kat, and Sofia would work with Snickers again.

Olivia told Grace that she would like to enter the driving classes, since they were the only events she could compete in without having to be pushed in her wheelchair.

"Why are there two driving classes?" Sofia still hoped she could enter one of them, even though she hadn't practiced driving as much as Olivia. But that wouldn't be fair to Olivia, would it?

"In youth driving, all the horses and their drivers compete in the show ring at the same time. The judge will tell them when to walk and trot and when to turn and change directions. At the end they'll line up and the judge will ask them to back up one at a time. The judge is interested in the way the horse moves and how it responds to the driver. If you really want a challenge, there's the driving obstacle class. People enter the ring one at a time and drive their horse through a pattern of maneuvers and obstacles just like you would in the halter obstacle class."

"I know I can do that," Olivia said. "I've been practicing all summer."

"You're ready for the challenge," Grace agreed. "And I'll be sitting next to you in the cart."

Olivia pursed her lips. "I don't need help—"

Grace threw up her hands. "Hey, Olivia, before you get yourself all worked up, it's a rule. All the kids must have an adult with them when they drive at this show. It's for safety."

"Oh," Olivia mumbled.

"And then there's jumper and hunter," Grace said. "You know about those classes already."

Olivia grabbed Sofia's hand. "You can push me like we practiced. We're going to do awesome."

A lump formed in Sofia's throat. Olivia was planning to enter both driving classes, and if Sofia didn't say anything now, she'd lose her chance to jump with Kit Kat. She swallowed hard. "I wonder if we could take turns. Like maybe you could do hunter and I could enter jumper by myself."

"Oh." Olivia's face fell.

What if she doesn't want to be my friend anymore?

Grace nodded. "I think that sounds fair, don't you, Olivia?"

Olivia closed her eyes and sighed. Then she straightened and smiled at Sofia. "I know it's hard work to push me around. You should do jumper in case we have to do a jump-off. You'll run a lot faster that way. And we want a win for the Mini Whinnies, don't we?"

Olivia didn't seem mad at Sofia, after all. They were a team. And they were going to win. Sofia wrapped her arms around Olivia. "We sure do!"

This is going to be the best horse show ever.

Chapter 22

Sofia swept the small pile of wood shavings and wisps of hay into a dustpan, then dumped the contents into a wheelbarrow. As she returned the broom to its hook on the wall beside the shovel and pitchforks, she admired the clean barn. She'd even managed to eliminate the cobwebs in the corners of the horses' stalls. Stephanie liked to keep things orderly, and often expressed frustration when others failed to return things to their proper locations. Since taking over most of the morning chores, Sofia had earned continual praise from both Stephanie and Grace.

Grace bounded through the door and swerved to avoid a collision with the wheelbarrow. "I've got a surprise for you. Close your eyes."

Sofia squeezed her eyes shut. "My birthday was two weeks ago, you know."

"Well, better late than never." Grace's boots squeaked on her way out the door. "No peeking."

"I'm not." Sofia couldn't imagine what Grace was planning to give her.

The footsteps returned. "Hold out your hands."

Sofia scrunched up her shoulders and extended her palms.

Grace laughed. "I promise it's not a snake or anything like that."

Soft material was pressed into her hands. *Clothing?*

"Okay, you can look now."

Sofia examined the stretchy shirt decorated with a purple and black swirly pattern. Gaudy rhinestones adorned the huge black collar. Smaller faux gemstones accented some of the black swirl designs along the front. Sofia couldn't imagine wearing this thing in public. People would stare at her. She looked up at Grace with a half-smile, not wanting to offend her.

"It's for the horse show," Grace said.

"Oh." She'd never been to a horse show before, but the pictures she'd seen featured girls in tan riding breeches, tall black boots, and plain white shirts with navy blazers.

"It's just a local club show, but many of the competitors will be wearing shirts like these, especially in the halter class," Grace said. "Do you have any black pants?"

"No." Sofia looked at her shoes. "But I have some birthday money, so I could buy some."

"You don't seem very sure about this. Are you nervous about the show?"

Sofia looked up, meeting Grace's eyes. "Yeah, a little. I guess I just... I didn't know that's what you wore to shows."

Grace nodded. "You think the shirt's a bit tacky, huh?"

"No, well..."

"I know you aren't into bling. That's okay. You don't have to wear it to school or anything." Grace laughed and brushed Sofia's shoulder. "I won many ribbons while wearing this, so maybe you can think of it as a lucky shirt. Plus, it's going to look awesome with Snickers' show halter."

"Thanks." Sofia held the shirt to her front. Maybe it wasn't so bad after all. If it helped her to win the halter class with Snickers...

"Whoa. Too bad I forgot my sunglasses." Olivia stood at the entrance of the barn, pointing at Sofia, then covering her eyes.

"Come on, it's not *that* bright," Grace said.

"It's my lucky shirt," Sofia said with a smile. "And I'm going to win all my classes."

Grace winked. "That's the spirit."

The members of the Mini Whinnies assembled around the picnic table. After calling the meeting to order, Grace said, "Before we groom the minis and practice for the horse show, I want to talk about what the judges will expect you and the horses to look like. The show we're going to isn't fancy, but you still need to dress appropriately."

"Do I need to wear a shirt like Sofia's?" Olivia asked. "I'm not sure if my eyes can handle it."

Ryan grinned at Sofia.

Grace sighed and shook her head. "Many of the girls will be wearing Western show shirts, but you don't have to wear one. A plain-colored, button-down shirt and nice pants will be fine, since you aren't in a showmanship class."

"But I'm in showmanship," said Ryan. "You said I should wear my suit."

"That's right," Grace said. "But for the other classes you don't need to dress up that much. You can take off the jacket and gloves."

Ryan nodded. "Mom's already helping me with the Little Miss Muffet costume. We found this awesome frilly pillow that I'm going to stick to my rear-end. You know, 'cause she sat on a tuffet."

Olivia rolled her eyes.

Sofia laughed. "What about eating your curds and whey?"

"Empty cottage cheese container. And I'm going to make the lead rope look like a spider's web."

"Brilliant," Grace said. "I'm glad at least one of you is thinking about how he's going to dress to impress. What do you think the horses' are going to need in order to be ready?"

"A bath?" Sofia asked. Snickers' white patches could certainly use some scrubbing.

"Absolutely. They will need to be clean and shiny. Anything else?"

Sofia looked at Olivia, who shrugged.

Grace glanced around the table. "No other ideas?" After an uncomfortable silence, she stood. "Ryan, can you go into the barn and get Kit Kat's halter and lead rope?"

"Sure." Ryan returned a moment later and gave them to Grace.

"Should we show Kit Kat in this?" Grace picked up the faded green halter. The top of the noseband had frayed and one of the buckles was slightly bent.

Sofia shook her head. "You told me Snickers has a show halter. Does Kit Kat?"

"We have special leather halters and lead ropes for both horses. And you'll be happy to know that they have lovely sliver accents to dazzle the judges. Now, Olivia, could you get Kit Kat and bring her here?"

"Yes, ma'am." Olivia shuffled over to the paddock. A few minutes later she returned with the mare.

Grace stroked Kit Kat's neck. "She's a beautiful girl, but she's not ready for the show ring yet." She pointed to the spiky section of mane behind the horse's ears and top of her neck. "Her bridle path needs to be shaved again. In fact, if we really want to do it right, we should clip their coats. Miniature horses tend to get a bit wooly-looking, even in the summer. It's a chore, but they'll look so sleek when we're done. And on the afternoon before the show, you'll need to give them a bath."

Ryan leaned close to Sofia and whispered, "I think we should accidentally soak Olivia with the hose."

"I heard that." Olivia glared at her brother. "If you do, you'll be sorry."

If they start fighting, I'll spray them both.

***

After parking her bike in Grampy's shed, Sofia hopped up the porch steps and flung open the screen door. "Hi Grampy! I'm – "

Grampy sat at the kitchen table, talking on the phone. He waved to Sofia and mouthed *your mother.* "Mandi, she's just walked in the door. Do you want to talk with her?"

Sofia hadn't spoken with Mom since the morning of her birthday two weeks ago. This was her chance to explain to her why she was wrong about Gramma Lisa. She needed to convince Mom to let her return before the start of school. Sofia had rehearsed the conversation many times since the sleepover at Olivia's house, but when she picked up the phone most of the speech fluttered out of her mind like a frightened bird.

"Hi, Mom."

"Honey Bear, it's so good to hear your voice."

Sofia held the receiver to her ear with one hand and jiggled the long, old-fashioned cord with the other. *Mom, you've got it wrong. Gramma Lisa never hurt me. I want to move back in with her.*

Instead Sofia said, "How are you?"

"Wonderful. England is beautiful. And we just got back from a trip to Paris. Can you believe that? Paul is amazing. So smart. So successful. I can't wait for you to meet him."

Sofia didn't care about Paul. She cared about Gramma Lisa and Sundance.

"Mom, I want to talk with you about what's going to happen after the summer's over." Sofia's heart pounded.

"I can't believe summer's more than half-way over. I'm sure you've been having tons of fun with Grampy. He told me that your friends took you to Funtown. You know, I went there, too, when I was a kid."

"I'm wondering," Sofia interrupted before her mother steered the conversation away from her urgent question, "what's going to happen after the summer ends. Why can't I—"

"Oh, Honey Bear! I have such a great surprise for you."

A surprise? Had Mom already made up with Gramma Lisa? Was she going to let Sofia move back to Connecticut after all?

"What's happening, Mom? Are you letting me –"

"I told you. It's a surprise. A wonderful, fantastic, incredible surprise."

Sofia blew out a frustrated breath. "Just tell me!"

"I want to tell you in person, Sofia." Mom chuckled. "It's the kind of surprise that's worth waiting for."

Sofia didn't want to wait. "When are you coming back, then?"

"Paul and I are flying into Boston late on the tenth of August. We'll sleep at a hotel and drive up to Grampy's the next day. I have so much to tell you about. We're going to be so happy."

They'd be arriving at Grampy's house on the day of the show. Maybe winning a blue ribbon would help Mom to realize how important horses were to her life. It might convince her that Sofia should be reunited with Sundance and Gramma Lisa even if Mom was still fighting with her.

"Mom, I'm going to be in a horse show that day. August eleventh. Can you come?"

"A horse show? Are you going with those little horses you told me about?"

"Yes, Snickers and Kit Kat."

"But you can't ride them. So what will you do with them at the horse show?"

"I'm going to be in halter, obstacle, and jumper. Olivia's going to drive Snickers. And Ryan's going to be in a costume class. He's dressing up like Little Miss Muffet and Kit Kat's going to be a spider."

Mom was silent for a moment. "That sounds...interesting."

"You can come, right Mom?"

"I'll try."

What do you mean, you'll try? "Mom, it's really important to me. I've been working on this all summer. You have to come."

"I need to check with Paul first."

Sofia balled her fist, but breathed deeply, trying to keep her voice steady. "The show starts at nine. Grampy can give you directions. Here, you can talk to him."

"Honey Bear, please listen. Paul might not—"

Sofia clenched the receiver so tightly it made her hand hurt. Maybe it would be better if Mom stayed in England forever with her smart, successful, rich boyfriend. "Bye, Mom."

Chapter 23

Sofia woke while it was still dark, too nervous and excited to fall back asleep before her alarm beeped at 5:15. She was about to compete in her first horse show, and Mom had promised to meet her there. At least that's what Mom had told Grampy, who planned to drive her and Paul to the show as soon as they arrived at his house. Sofia would finally learn Mom's news.

On the road in the Murphy's van, Olivia leaned against Sofia's shoulder, snoring softly. Ryan's neck and head slumped forward, bobbing as the vehicle bumped along the winding country road.

When Mom watches me at the show, she'll see how much I love horses, and how I need to be with Sundance. Then I'll convince Mom to make up with Gramma Lisa. Of course, that would mean saying goodbye to Snickers and Kit Kat and Olivia and Ryan and Grace and... no, she couldn't think about that now.

Adrenaline shot through Sofia as Stephanie's horse trailer in front of them slowed and turned left into the showground's entrance. "We're here!"

Olivia jerked awake.

Ryan yawned and dragged his hand across his face, wiping drool from the corner of his mouth. "What time is it?"

Pastor Amy turned toward the backseat. "8:25. You still have plenty of time to get your numbers before the show starts." She unzipped a small cooler and took out three bottles of water. "Make sure you drink this. I don't want you kids getting dehydrated."

Olivia elbowed Sofia and rolled her eyes.

Sofia grinned and uncapped her bottle, taking a sip. *There's no way I'm going to let myself get heat-stroke today.*

David steered the van around a pothole, following Stephanie's truck and trailer down a dirt road. They passed a dozen parked trailers. A heavy-set woman unloaded a young palomino and tied him beside two pinto horses. An older couple reclined in lawn chairs under a pop-up sun shelter. A teenage boy held a phone in one hand and a long lead rope in the other, staring at the screen while his buckskin miniature horse grazed.

Stephanie parked in a sandy area beside a large pine tree. Grace jumped out of the passenger side and waved in the direction of the Murphy's vehicle.

David eased the van into a spot beside the horse trailer and turned off the engine. "I know you three are going to make me proud today. Remember, good sportsmanship is more important than winning."

"We're going to have excellent sportsmanship *and* blue ribbons today, Dad." Olivia reached for her crutches and slid open the door.

Sofia followed. Her legs felt stiff from the long car ride, yet her body jittered with anticipation.

Grace tossed a lead rope to Sofia. "You can unload Snickers. I'll take Kit Kat."

Ryan frowned. "What about me?"

"I need you to wrestle open the door. It sticks sometimes. And it's heavy."

Ryan flexed his arm muscles. "I'm the man for the job."

He struggled with the bolt latches, which groaned as they slid open. Ryan grunted as he lowered the door to the ground. It became a ramp for the horses to exit the trailer.

Snickers whinnied and turned his head, looking behind his shoulder. Sofia could see the whites of his eyes. "It's okay, boy."

Grace nodded to Sofia. "You can unload him now. Just watch your footing." She pointed to the piles of wet manure staining the trailer floor.

"Eww." Ryan wrinkled his nose.

Sofia entered a side door near Snickers' head. Stroking his neck, she attached the lead to his halter and unclipped the trailer tie. "Let's get out of here."

Snickers let out another ear-splitting neigh before scrambling backward.

"Whoa!" Sofia struggled to keep up with him.

"Well, I guess that's one way to do it," Grace said as she backed Kit Kat down the ramp.

"He's kind of sweaty," Sofia said. Then she noticed the brown streaks dripping between his hind legs. Some of the hairs at the bottom of his tail were no longer white. "And he has..."

Grace handed Kit Kat to Stephanie and inspected Snickers. "He hasn't gone to a show or ridden in a trailer for a few years. He must be nervous. Why don't you walk him around a little, and let him get used to the place. Then we can wash him up and brush him again."

Sofia nodded. Her stomach fluttered. *Snickers needs me to be calm.* She inhaled deeply and let out a slow breath.

"Mom, can you hold Kit Kat while I take Ryan and Olivia to the show office to get their numbers?" Grace asked. "We'll get Sofia's number, too."

"Certainly." Stephanie led the mare to a grassy area across the dirt path.

Snickers whinnied a third time as he pranced in Kit Kat's direction. Sofia pulled on his lead. "No grass for you. Let's check out the show ring."

A white, three-railed fence outlined the rectangular arena, which was at least four times the size of Snickers and Kit Kat's paddock. Olivia should have plenty of room to maneuver Snickers in the cart, even with several other competitors in the ring.

A shack-like building with a huge window overlooking the show ring stood on her left. A girl about Sofia's age exited the door, clutching a white paper. Her glossy brown hair flowed behind her as she bounded down the steps to ground level. A moment later, a woman appeared in the doorway and followed her down the stairs.

The girl waved and approached Sofia. "I've never seen you before. What's your horse's name?"

"Snickers."

The girl stretched out her hand to pet Snickers' nose. "Hi, Snickers. I love your eyes."

"Julia, who's your new friend?" the woman called out.

"Snickers."

The woman sighed loudly. "I was referring to the girl, not the horse."

Julia shrugged.

"I'm Sofia."

The woman extended her hand. "Nice to meet you. I'm Catherine, and this is my daughter, Julia. You must be new to this club."

"It's my first horse show," Sofia admitted.

Snickers lunged toward a patch of long, green grass, snatching a mouthful.

"No!" Sofia yanked him away and tugged the grass out of his mouth, leaving her hands coated in frothy green slime.

Julia smirked. "Looks like you don't have very good control over your horse. And he's got poop stains on his legs."

Heat rose in Sofia's cheeks.

"Julia, please," Catherine said. "Don't be rude." She turned to Sofia. "You might want to clean him up a bit, though. And don't be afraid to tell him you're the boss."

Sofia bit her lip as Julia and Catherine turned and walked away. "Come on, Snickers." She brushed her stinging eyes with the front of her dirty hand and led Snickers back to the trailer.

***

Sofia and Olivia settled into lawn chairs beside the show ring fence as Ryan and Kit Kat prepared for their showmanship class. Grace, Pastor

Amy, and David stood behind them. Stephanie held Snickers, watching from a short distance away.

"Go, Ryan!" Olivia called to her brother.

Ryan smiled back at them as the judge inspected the bay mare two horses over from Kit Kat.

Sofia would never admit this to Ryan, but she thought he looked handsome in his suit and cowboy hat, in a brotherly sort of way, of course. When had she started thinking of him as being like a brother instead of simply being Olivia's brother?

Kit Kat stood perfectly still, her ears pricked forward. As the judge approached the mare, Ryan moved to the opposite side in the way Grace had taught him. The judge inspected both horse and handler, jotting notes onto a clipboard before moving to the next horse.

Julia. Sofia's hand-me-down show shirt looked downright plain compared with Julia's hot pink, sliver, and black, spangled jacket and matching pants. The gelding by her side gleamed in the bright sunlight. Sofia had to admit that her horse was stunning, with his polished black hooves and a blindingly white coat sprinkled with black spots. She remembered this pattern was called leopard appaloosa.

The judge examined her clipboard again, and conferred with the ring steward before handing him her notes. He entered the building next to the ring. A minute later, he returned with a handful of ribbons.

A woman's voice crackled through a speaker mounted on the side of the building. "The results for youth showmanship, ages 8-12 are as follows. In sixth place, number 235, Aiden Dube, with Stonybrook Farm Dreamweaver."

Aiden frowned as he received his green rosette. Sofia felt sorry for the small boy, who looked even younger than eight. He'd placed last in this class of six. With slumped shoulders, he led his bay mare out of the ring.

The woman on the loudspeaker announced fifth place. Fourth. Third. Ryan and Julia were the only two left.

"In second place, number 122, Ryan Murphy, with Candy Ridge Truly Scrumptious."

"Candy Ridge Truly Scrumptious?" Olivia shook her head.

Grace laughed. "That's her registered name. Kit Kat's her barn name."

Ryan grinned as he received his red ribbon. He exited the ring while "Number 146, Julia Blackstone-Hill, with Show Me the Razzle Dazzle" claimed her blue.

Julia waved the ribbon over her head. "Woo hoo, Razzy! We're the best."

Sofia scrunched up her face, frustrated that Ryan hadn't beaten Julia.

"You did fantastic!" Pastor Amy hugged Ryan. "Second place in your first ever show."

David took out his phone. "Come on, Olivia, get in the picture with your brother."

"Sofia, too," said Ryan.

"Why don't you all get in for a family photo?" Grace asked. "I'll take one."

Sofia swallowed the lump forming in her throat and forced a smile for the camera. Pastor Amy and David, Olivia and Ryan. They were a family. But where was her family? She scanned the crowd, searching for Mom and Grampy. *Shouldn't they be here by now?*

Chapter 24

Fourteen halter classes. It was one thing to see them listed on a piece of paper. It was quite another to wait through all of them. An hour and a half had passed since Ryan's debut in showmanship, and there were still two more classes before Sofia and Snickers were scheduled to enter the show ring.

Snickers tugged a mouthful of hay from the bag tied to the side of the trailer. She and Grace had scrubbed off his sweat and manure stains, and he appeared relaxed. It was Sofia who was a bundle of nerves.

She glanced at her phone for what seemed to be the hundredth time. Almost eleven o'clock. No sign of Grampy and Mom. If they didn't get here soon, they'd miss her first class.

Stephanie tapped Sofia on the shoulder. "It's time for you and Snickers to get ready. They'll be calling your class in about five minutes, I think."

Olivia looked up from the book she was reading. "You're going to do great. And you haven't blinded me yet with that shirt you're wearing."

It's not as flashy as Julia's. Sofia tugged at her sleeve and brushed a stray curl out of her eyes. "Can you hold my phone?"

"Sure. I'll even take pictures." Olivia reached for the phone.

It chirped. A text from Grampy.

"Your mom just left Boston. She and Paul will go directly to the show. I'm leaving now, and should be there in a little more than an hour. Love you."

"Are you okay, Sofia?" Pastor Amy asked.

Sofia's stomach churned. "I guess," she mumbled. "Grampy's on his way. But I don't know when Mom will get here."

Stephanie reached for Sofia's shoulder and pulled her into a hug. "Don't worry about that now. We're here, and we're going to cheer you

143

on. You and Snickers have a job to do. Now go out there and make us proud."

Sofia led Snickers to the arena. Stephanie was right. She couldn't think about Mom.

Four other competitors had gathered by the entrance. The ring steward opened the gate, and a girl entered the arena with her black and white pinto.

The horses were supposed to enter the halter class at a trot. Snickers apparently had a different idea. He lifted his head, snorted, and took a step backward.

"Come on," Sofia muttered through clenched teeth.

"Looks like you still don't have control over your horse," Julia taunted under her breath. "Let's go, Razzy. We've got another blue ribbon with our names on it." She and Show Me the Razzle Dazzle pushed past them through the gate and entered into the ring at a brisk trot.

Sofia tugged the leather lead connected to Snickers' flashy show halter. His coat gleamed. He had never looked so beautiful, but that wouldn't do anything for him if he refused to enter the ring. Of course, maybe it would be better if he didn't. Then she wouldn't embarrass herself in front of all these people. Sofia thought she might throw up.

But she couldn't give up, not with Olivia and Ryan and Grace and Stephanie cheering for her. *Mom's not here, though.* How long did it take to drive up here from Boston? Hours, probably.

She and Snickers were the only competitors still outside the gate. Taking a deep breath, Sofia plunged forward. Snickers followed, lagging two steps behind.

They jogged past the judge and joined the line-up. Sofia halted Snickers and encouraged him to stand as Grace had taught them, with his feet square. He stepped sideways. Hands shaking with nerves, she tried to reposition him, but Snickers backed up instead.

Sofia glanced at Julia. Her horse stood at attention, his neck arched forward and his ears alert. She replayed Julia's words again and again. *"Looks like you don't have control over your horse."*

Snickers whinnied. And then, to Sofia's horror, he lifted his tail and pooped.

Her mind raced, assaulting her with her deepest fears. *Why did you think you could do this? You're going to come in last place. You're letting the Mini Whinnies down. Mom will never let you see Sundance again. Nobody loves you.*

Sofia shook her head. She needed to focus. She moved Snickers forward a step to square up his front legs. She snapped her fingers, hoping he would lift his head and stretch his neck like the other horses were doing.

The judge stood in front of them now. She wrote something down and moved to the next horse.

Sofia's heart hammered as she waited for the announcer's voice.

"The results for youth halter, ages 8-12, multi-color geldings are as follows: In fifth place, number 117, Sofia Ruiz, with Candy Ridge Sweet Dreams."

Sofia hissed out a breath she didn't realize she was holding. Fifth place out of five horses. She and Snickers walked forward to receive their pink ribbon. She wanted to throw it and grind it into the ground.

Of course, Julia won the class. Again. Sofia glared at the snotty girl and her perfect horse as they received their second blue ribbon of the day.

***

Sofia slumped into one of Pastor Amy's folding beach chairs. This horse show was a disaster.

Pastor Amy touched Sofia's shoulder. "Do you want something to eat? There might be a peanut butter and jelly sandwich left. And there are a few egg salad sandwiches."

Sofia shook her head.

"A granola bar? Maybe an apple?" Pastor Amy smiled, but concern shone through her eyes. "What about a drink?"

"Water, I guess." Sofia wasn't sure her stomach could handle even that right now.

She stared at the paper on her lap. It showed the pattern she needed to memorize for the halter obstacle class. It didn't look that complicated, but she'd probably find a way to mess up. Either that, or Snickers would decide that an invisible troll lived under the wooden bridge he was expected to walk over.

Looks like you don't have control over your horse. Would Julia compete in that class too? Probably.

Grace, Ryan, and Olivia scrambled to assemble Kit Kat's spider costume. Ryan had already dressed in his Little Miss Muffet outfit, complete with a bright yellow wig and frilly hat. The tuffet had been tossed onto the chair beside Sofia, ready to be pinned onto Ryan's rear-end as soon as they managed to secure the pool noodle "legs" to the straps around Kit Kat's belly. Everyone seemed to be having a great time. Everyone but Sofia.

Stomach churning, she reached into her pocket for her phone. A glance confirmed what she already knew. No updates about Mom and Paul. With lunch break nearly over, it wouldn't be long before she and Snickers went back into the ring.

Sofia jumped as a heavy hand tapped her on the top of her head.

"Sorry, I didn't mean to startle you."

"Grampy," Sofia moaned, leaping to her feet and falling into his arms. Her lower jaw trembled as she fought to keep the tears from spilling from the corners of her eyes, but she couldn't hold them back.

"Oh, Sofia," Grampy said, patting her back. "I'm sorry your mother isn't here yet."

Sofia hugged Grampy harder. "I'm glad you came, though," she said through shuddering breaths.

"She's had a bit of a rough morning," Pastor Amy said.

"What happened?" Grampy released Sofia and stepped back.

Sofia shook her head. She didn't want to talk about it.

"Is this yours?" Grampy picked up the fifth place ribbon Sofia had tossed under her chair.

"Yeah." Sofia looked away. "But don't get too excited. I came in last place."

"It's a pretty color, anyway." Grampy turned the ribbon over in his hands. "Are you upset because of losing, or because your mother's not here yet?"

Both. Sofia rubbed her tear-stained cheeks and swallowed. "I don't know."

Pastor Amy brushed Sofia's arm. "She's done a great job, but her horse has been acting up a bit."

"It's not his fault." Sofia knew that Pastor Amy was trying to be nice, but her comment made her feel prickly inside. "He was nervous. We both were."

Sofia remembered how nervous she'd been when she was learning to trot on Sundance. She'd felt so out of control, as her bottom was tossed high off the saddle with every stride. After a minute of her bouncing and clutching his mane, her horse slowed and halted. She kicked his sides, but wouldn't budge. Gramma Lisa told her that horses can read your feelings better than people can. If you're upset or fearful, they'll sense it, and think something must be wrong. When Sofia relaxed, Sundance did what she asked.

Sofia's nerves and negative thoughts were only reinforcing Snickers' fears. He needed her to be a calm and confident leader.

Julia was wrong. Sofia did have control. It was time to stop moping about, feeling sorry for herself. Snickers needed her.

Chapter 25

Ryan stood beside Kit Kat, clutching the blue ribbon he'd won in the costume class. Too bad Julia hadn't entered. Sofia would have loved to see Ryan beat her. No matter. In a few minutes she would compete against Julia in the halter obstacle, and she would wipe the smirk off that snotty girl's face.

Kit Kat and Ryan would be competing, too. Sofia hoped they did well. Second place would be good. First place belonged to her and Snickers.

As the participants of the halter obstacle class gathered by the gate to walk the course with the judge, Julia's hot-pink, silver, and black outfit sparkled in the sunlight. Sofia tried not to look at her. *Pay attention to the judge. Forget about Julia.*

After their practice walk-through, Sofia and Ryan exchanged nervous smiles.

Stephanie led Snickers to Sofia and handed her his lead rope. "You've got this."

The first person to enter the ring was the tiny boy named Aiden who had placed last during showmanship. His mare obediently trotted over three poles on the ground, but balked at the wooden bridge. Aiden looped around for a second try, but his horse skidded sideways and tried to walk around the platform. On their third attempt, the horse stepped up and walked across as if she had navigated the obstacle a hundred times before. When the pair completed the course, the spectators politely clapped.

The loudspeaker squealed with the announcer's booming voice. "Next up is number 117, Sofia Ruiz with Candy Ridge Sweet Dreams."

Olivia transferred both crutches into one hand and gave Sofia a one-armed hug. "Good luck. I know you'll do great."

A tall man in a cowboy hat opened the metal gate.

Sofia patted Snickers' neck before leading him to the entrance of the show arena. She took a deep breath and exhaled slowly. Her heart raced, but at least her hands felt steady. The judge nodded to her, signaling that she could begin the course.

Six obstacles.

Sofia urged Snickers into a trot, hoping this wouldn't be a repeat of their disastrous performance in the halter class. *I must be a calm and confident leader.* Snickers obeyed, keeping pace with Sofia.

Three brightly-painted poles lay on the ground before them. Snickers needed to trot evenly over the center of each one without losing his momentum. Over the first, the second, the third, and they were through.

She slowed her horse to a walk as they approached the next obstacle. The narrow bridge didn't have a railing, and the judge had told them it would be safer for the handler to stay on the ground while their horse walked over it. Sofia bit her lip. Would Snickers step onto the platform without her showing him how?

Snickers halted in front of the bridge.

"It's okay, boy." Sofia tried to sound calm and comforting, though her heart thudded in her throat.

The pinto placed his front left hoof onto the wood. Then his right. *So far, so good.* Sofia urged him forward. He lifted a hind foot and placed it onto the obstacle.

"There you go. One more step."

All four of Snickers' feet were now on the platform. Sofia walked forward and her horse followed. Snickers reached the end of the bridge and hesitated. Then he leapt off, nearly yanking the lead rope from Sofia's hands. He landed a few feet from the bridge. *That's probably the biggest jump he's ever made. Too bad it's in the wrong event.* Even though he would lose a few points for not stepping down properly, Sofia couldn't help smiling.

At the next obstacle, Snickers was expected to back through poles arranged in an L shape. They had practiced backing many times before, and Snickers completed the task without stepping outside of the lines.

Looming ahead of them was a plastic curtain, hanging from a rod that was supported on each end by vertical poles. The curtain had been cut into numerous lengths, creating ribbons of plastic that fluttered in the breeze. Both she and Snickers were supposed to walk under and through the streamers.

Sofia needed to act like walking through flapping plastic was a perfectly normal thing to expect horses to do, even if it smacked them in the face. She took a steadying breath and strode forward.

Snickers lifted his head and pricked his ears. Sofia could see his muscles tensing in preparation to spook.

"Nothing to worry about," she whispered, and walked under the curtain.

Snickers rushed through it, as if afraid that if he lingered, a terrifying monster might bite his butt. Perhaps the judge would knock a few points off of their score, but Sofia smiled. They had made it through the hardest two obstacles.

Next they trotted through a simple pattern of cones. They were spaced closely together, which made it difficult to weave through without slowing to a walk, but Sofia led Snickers with confidence. They trotted through without knocking a single one. Surely they would receive a high score.

Only one more obstacle!

Sofia positioned Snickers' front feet inside a hula hoop. She raised it slowly up his legs, and then moved the top of the hoop up his neck and over his head. Thankfully, Snickers did not have to know how to twirl a hula hoop around his belly, though that would have been a cool trick. All Sofia had to do was pass it over his back, down his hind legs and to the ground. Success! She led Snickers forward while the hoop remained on the ground.

They passed between the pair of cones marking the finish line. People clapped. The tall man with a cowboy hat opened the gate, and they exited the ring. Sofia refused to look at Julia, who leaned against the fence.

Grace gave Sofia a high-five. "That was amazing!"

Stephanie pulled Sofia into a fierce hug. "I thought Snickers was going to spook at the curtain, but you led him right through. I'm so proud of you."

Grampy beamed. "Look at you. What a fine young horseman you are."

"Horsewoman," Olivia said, slapping Sofia on the back.

The announcer called Julia and her appaloosa gelding into the ring. Sofia didn't want to watch.

"Grampy, can you take a picture of me and Snickers?"

Grampy fished his new cell phone from his pocket and stared at the screen. "How do you do that, again?"

Sofia smiled. "I'll show you."

The spectators applauded as Julia exited the ring.

"Oh, darling!" Julia's mother rushed to her side. "You were perfect."

"I know." Julia wrinkled her nose at Sofia as she passed.

Sofia balled her fists.

A girl named Emily competed next, with her black and white pinto that had been in Sofia's halter class. Her horse had no problem going over the bridge, but refused to go through the curtain. After four unsuccessful attempts, the judge moved her on to the next obstacle.

Ryan jogged in place. "You're lucky that you got to go early," he said to Sofia. "I'm getting more and more nervous watching all the things that could go wrong."

Olivia shrugged. "Come on. You have the calmest, best-trained horse at this show. Nothing bothers Kit Kat."

Emily and her pinto finished the course, and the announcer called Ryan into the ring.

"Wish me luck," he said.

Ryan didn't need luck, however. Olivia was right. Kit Kat navigated every obstacle like she had practiced it for months. Ryan could have done a better job with guiding her through the L shape. Kit Kat's feet clipped the side of the poles twice as she backed through. But considering that two months ago Ryan had been afraid of horses, his performance was incredible.

Sofia and Grampy clapped. Olivia whooped. David whistled. Pastor Amy jumped up and down. And Ryan took a bow.

The ring steward consulted with the judge for a minute and retreated into the show office. He returned with ribbons.

"The results for halter obstacle, ages 8 to 12 are as follows," declared the invisible person over the loudspeakers. "In fifth place, number 248, Emily Simpson, with Hocus Pocus."

The ring steward gave the pink ribbon to Emily, who looked like she might break into tears. Sofia knew how she felt.

"In fourth place, number 235, Aiden Dube, with Stonybrook Farm Dreamweaver."

Sofia smiled as Aiden received his white ribbon, glad that he hadn't come in last place again.

When her name was called for third place, Sofia felt a twinge of jealousy that Ryan had beaten her. Ryan had an easier horse, and Sofia might have won the class if she'd competed with Kit Kat instead of Snickers. But she was also proud that she'd been able to overcome her anxiety and steady Snickers' nerves. After receiving the yellow ribbon, she crossed her fingers, hoping Ryan would beat Julia.

The announcer crushed Sofia's wish. "In second place, number 122, Ryan Murphy, with Candy Ridge Truly Scrumptious."

Ryan nodded, accepting the result, and took his red rosette.

"And winning this class is number 146, Julia Blackstone-Hill, with Show Me the Razzle Dazzle."

Julia pumped her fist into the air and trotted with her horse to receive their ribbon. "Three blues in a row, Razzy!" She waved her blue ribbon at Sofia as she exited the ring.

Sofia clenched her teeth. She had to beat this snobby girl.

While the teenagers and adults competed in their halter obstacle divisions, Sofia studied the pattern of jumps for the hunter class. The course was simple enough. What concerned her was the right-hand turn after the second jump, which would require speeding up and pushing Olivia's wheelchair around the outside of Kit Kat's path. It was Olivia's responsibility to signal when to turn and to direct the horse to move away from her wheelchair, but a lot could go wrong. They'd worked on this move at home, but today's experience with Snickers reminded Sofia that horses don't always behave the way you'd expect, especially when their handlers are nervous.

Olivia snatched the hunter course directions from Sofia's hand.

"Hey, I'm still looking at that," Sofia protested.

"You've got that thing memorized by now. Plus, you're not the one who needs to know it. I'm the one showing. You're just pushing the wheelchair where I tell you."

Sofia pursed her lips. They had practiced together for weeks, but Olivia was making it sound like it didn't matter who pushed her. Maybe she should suggest that Ryan take her place. *Let's see how she likes that!* But a fight with Olivia was the last thing she wanted right now.

Pastor Amy cleared her throat. "Olivia, I know you're feeling nervous, but that doesn't give you an excuse to be rude."

"I'm not – "

Grace jumped up from her chair and pointed to the show arena. "Looks like you two need to get ready. They just started the little kid's hunter, and your class is next."

"Do I really have to do the walk-through in the wheelchair?" Olivia whined.

Sofia let out a frustrated breath.

"Yes, you do," Grace said. "So Sofia can get a feel for what it will be like to push you on that surface."

Grace bent her knees and placed her hands on Olivia's shoulders, looking directly into Olivia's eyes. "If you want to win this class, you need to start thinking like a winner. That means you stop feeling sorry for yourself and recognize that you have something none of the other kids are going to have. You've got a best-friend who will be right there with you in the ring. I suggest you show her a bit more respect and appreciation."

"I'm..." Olivia stared at the ground. "I'm sorry. I know I couldn't do it without you, Sofia. We're a team." She wiped her eyes.

"So let's go be a team," Sofia said. "And let's beat Julia while we're at it."

Olivia eased herself into the wheelchair and handed her crutches to Pastor Amy. "That girl doesn't stand a chance against us."

As they approached the show ring entrance, Julia stared, open-mouthed, at Sofia. "What are you doing?" She pointed to Olivia's wheelchair.

"Pushing my friend." Sofia glared at Julia.

The other competitors were gathering by the gate, preparing to walk the course with the judge. Aiden and Emily were there, along with two other girls and a tall boy. They didn't make eye contact with Sofia or Olivia. Even with Julia making a fuss, the others pretended Olivia was invisible.

Sofia remembered what Olivia had told her on the night of her sleepover. She wanted to scream at the others. *Look at us!*

Julia scrunched her face. "She's going to be in this class?"

Olivia shrugged. "Looks like it."

"What's wrong with her?" Julia looked like she'd just eaten a sour pickle.

Sofia opened her mouth, ready to blurt out *What's wrong with you,* when Olivia pointed at Julia's rhinestone encrusted jacket.

"I'm blind," she said. "Your outfit burned out my eyeballs."

Sofia snatched her hand away from the wheelchair's handle, biting her fist in a vain attempt to stifle her laughter. A moment later, she doubled over.

The tall boy nodded to Olivia and grinned. Emily covered her mouth. The two other girls elbowed each other. And after glancing at Julia as if to confirm she wouldn't see him, Aiden whispered, "good one."

Julia spun on her heels and stomped away from the other competitors.

Sofia grinned at her friend. Olivia was no longer invisible.

Chapter 26

Aiden and his bay mare were the first to jump the hunter course. Sofia silently rooted for him, but Aiden's bad luck continued. His horse refused the first jump, knocked over the second, and slammed on the brakes just before the third jump. Sofia thought his mare would refuse to go over, but a moment later she sprang up, cleared the fence, and completed the rest of course with no further mistakes.

Emily's black and white pinto enthusiastically raced through the course, while Emily struggled to keep up with him. As he lunged forward at the last jump, Emily stumbled and lost her grip on his lead rope, and the gelding broke free. He galloped through the finishing cones, skidding to a stop inches from the gate. They were disqualified. It looked like Emily was having even worse luck than Aiden.

Sofia swallowed hard. Kit Kat was a talented jumper. Would her luck change? *We've got to beat Julia.*

The tall boy went next, leading a plump grey gelding. His horse slowed to a walk after each jump. Sofia thought they both looked rather bored, but they stayed together, and they didn't accumulate any faults.

Then the announcer called Julia and Razz into the ring. Sofia hoped the gelding would knock over a pole, but he cleared each obstacle, navigating the course smoothly at a brisk trot. Razz broke into a canter for a few strides between one of the jumps, which could count against them. It was still possible for Olivia and Kit Kat to beat her – if they had a perfect round.

As Julia led her horse through the gate, she smirked at Sofia.

Sofia squeezed the handles of Olivia's wheelchair and glared back.

"Next up, number 268, Olivia Murphy with Candy Ridge Truly Scrumptious."

"Are you ready?" asked Olivia.

Sofia's heart pounded. "I hope so."

"Come on. We need some team spirit. You ready?"

"Yes!" Sofia shouted.

"Then let's show them how it's done."

As Sofia pushed her friend through the gate, Kit Kat walking confidently by Olivia's side, she noticed that the number of spectators standing along the fence had grown considerably. People lined up two-deep in places. Strangers were pointing their phones and cameras at them. Many were clapping.

Sofia took a deep breath and exhaled slowly. She couldn't think about an audience. She had a job to do.

"Trot," Olivia commanded.

Sofia pushed.

"Left. Now straight."

Kit Kat trotted evenly toward the first jump and cleared it in perfect form. The second jump was only a few strides away. Sofia felt a trickle of sweat run down her back.

Olivia lifted her arm, and the tiny mare leapt up and over, her red coat shimmering in the sunlight.

And here was the dreaded right-hand turn. She waited for Olivia to call out "right turn" before thrusting the wheelchair in a wide arc. She had to move faster than Kit Kat, while Olivia kept the mare at a steady pace to her right. Sofia's breaths were coming faster now.

"Straight," Olivia said.

A white box filled with plastic flowers had been positioned under the third jump. Kit Kat soared over it, her front hooves tucked neatly under her chest.

Olivia called for a left-hand turn, which was much easier because Kit Kat had to go around the outside of the circle this time. They cleared two more jumps, followed by another left-hand turn.

Sofia tried to ignore the crowd, who'd begun cheering wildly. One more jump. The flower-box again.

Sweat stung Sofia's eyes, and she tried to blink it away. A cramp bit at her side. Her arms felt like jelly, and her calf muscles burned, but she couldn't stop now. She pushed through the pain.

Kit Kat flew over the last jump. *Perfect!* Sofia wanted to shout.

Olivia waited until they passed through the finish line before raising her hands into the air. The crowd exploded with whoops and applause.

As they exited the arena, a woman approached them with tears in her eyes. "That was the most amazing thing I've ever seen."

Three more women pressed into them, reaching out to touch Olivia's shoulders and hands. "You are such an inspiration," one said, before turning to Sofia. "And dear, you did a marvelous job, too. You worked together so well."

"Excuse me," Stephanie said, pushing against the growing crowd of admirers as she made her way to Sofia and Olivia. "I'm sure they'll be happy to give you their autographs after the show is over."

Olivia and Sofia laughed in unison.

The loudspeaker squealed. "Please clear the gate area. This class is still in progress."

Sofia watched the remaining two horses complete the course, barely daring to breathe. One clipped a hind hoof against the fourth jump, sending the pole skittering to the ground. The other horse spooked at the flowers, dragging his handler around the jump and missing it entirely.

Sofia paced in a wide circle as she awaited the results.

The loudspeaker squealed. As each place was called, Sofia crossed her fingers. Seventh, sixth, fifth, fourth... "In third, number 178, Caitlin Legender, with Fly Me to the Moon." It was down to Olivia and Julia.

"In second place, 146, Julia Blackstone-Hill, with Show Me the Razzle Dazzle."

Ryan jumped up and down. "You won!"

Julia shot Sofia a poisonous look and stomped forward to receive her ribbon.

But Sofia didn't care anymore. "We did it!" She hugged Olivia.

"And winning the class is number 268, Olivia Murphy with Candy Ridge Truly Scrumptious."

The crowd erupted in applause as Olivia shuffled forward with her crutches, having ditched her wheelchair at the first possible moment. After receiving her blue ribbon she raised it into the air.

"That's not fair!" Julia protested loudly. "The only reason she won is because the judge felt sorry for her."

Julia's mother shook her head and put a finger to her lips, but Julia shook her fists. "All she did is sit in that stupid chair and get pushed around. She didn't do anything."

Sofia narrowed her eyes and stepped toward Julia. "You stuck up –"

Grampy clamped his hand over Sofia's shoulder. "That's enough."

"But – "

"You're bigger than that, Sofia." Grampy pointed to the crowd surrounding Olivia and her family. "You and Olivia inspired all these people. I bet they've never seen anything like what you two did. You won fair and square. Just let it be."

Chapter 27

Sofia fidgeted with the end of Kit Kat's lead rope, spinning it in alternating directions while the mare nibbled on a sparse patch of grass. Her final class was about to begin. This would be her last chance to win her own blue ribbon. And Mom was about to miss it. *Where could she be?*

Julia stood nearby, stroking Razz's elegant neck and refusing to make eye contact with Sofia. Grampy was right. It didn't matter what Julia said. Everyone knew that she and Olivia had beaten Julia fair and square. Could Sofia beat her again?

The jumps had been arranged in a different pattern from the hunter class, and some had been raised in height, with the flower jump the tallest. Having a beautiful horse and a fancy outfit wouldn't help Julia in this event. All that mattered was clearing the jumps, and Sofia knew that Kit Kat could sail over every one of them.

Sofia glanced at her phone before handing it to Grampy. Mom didn't know that she even had a cell phone, so why did she feel the urge to check for a message from her?

Mom and Paul should have arrived by now. She wanted Mom to see her compete, but the more she thought about it, the more anxious she felt. What if she forgot the pattern or tripped over her own feet and came in last place again? She could imagine Mom saying *Oh Honey Bear, you were so cute. Who cares what place you got as long as you had fun?*

Horses were more than fun. They were her life. She had to convince Mom of this, to prove to her that she was meant to be with Sundance. It was unfair that Mom's fight with Gramma Lisa had ripped her away from him.

Sofia jumped as the announcer called Caitlin and her palomino to the ring. She needed to keep her mind focused on winning this class.

Caitlin's horse refused the flower jump, running around it rather than over it, resulting in a penalty of four faults.

Emily's speedy pinto flew over each jump without knocking anything down. Zero faults. They'd be tough competitors in a jump-off.

Sofia clapped when Aiden and his mare trotted through the finish line having also jumped a clean round. He was now tied with Emily for first place.

Three more competitors took their turns, but all of them finished with faults. They would not be advancing to a timed jump-off.

When the announcer called Sofia's name, Grampy patted her on the back, Ryan wished her luck, and Olivia insisted that she didn't need luck because they all knew that she had the best horse at the show.

Sofia wiped her sweaty palms across the front of her pants and led Kit Kat into the arena. It was time to show Julia Blackstone-Hill that Sofia Ruiz had control of her horse.

She jogged forward and Kit Kat trotted calmly beside her. Speed wasn't important – yet. She needed a perfect round to tie with Emily and Aiden so she could advance to the jump-off.

They turned to the left, cleared the first jump, and moved diagonally across the ring to the big flower jump. The tiny mare leapt over with ease.

A few yards later she guided Kit Kat to the right, approaching a line of two jumps with three strides between. No problem. Next, a sweeping right turn and back over the flower jump. Sofia breathed hard as they rounded the turn for the two remaining jumps. Up and over. Trot, trot. Up and over. A clean round.

Sofia and Kit Kat were now in a three-way tie for first place. She was still inhaling deep gulps of air when Julia and Show Me the Razzle Dazzle made it a four-way.

Grace, Olivia, and Ryan crowded around her, offering last-minute tips and words of encouragement.

"You're gonna win," Olivia insisted, waving one of her crutches for emphasis.

"I don't know. Emily's horse is really fast," Sofia said.

"Yes, but she doesn't have good control. Remember how he got away from her in the last class?" Grace said. "You'll need speed and control, especially through the turns."

"That rude girl's got a good horse, too," said Ryan.

Olivia glared at him.

He shrugged. "Not as good as Kit Kat, of course."

"And Sofia's going to win." Olivia patted Sofia's shoulder.

Sofia nodded, wishing she shared Olivia's confidence.

The jumps had been raised higher. The scoring remained the same, but if any of the competitors tied, the one with the fastest time would win.

Speed. Control. Tight turns.

Aiden's horse jumped well until she clipped a hind hoof against a pole. It wobbled in its cup, as if deciding whether it wanted to remain in place. It chose to fall. Four faults.

As Emily and her pinto raced through the course at a canter, Sofia noticed they wasted precious seconds on each turn, especially the tricky right-hand ones. The horse would surge ahead of her and she struggled to bring him under control, but they finished with a clean round. Sofia would have to beat their time.

Sofia scanned the clusters of spectators lining the arena. No sign of Mom. "Come on, Kit Kat," she whispered as she led her back into the show ring. She urged the tiny, chestnut mare into a brisk trot and passed through the starting cones.

The next forty-seven seconds passed in a blur of motion and thought. Control through the tight turns. Speed through the straight areas. They flew out of the final turn and broke into a canter, Sofia running as fast as her legs would take her. Kit Kat bounded over the final two jumps, and they galloped across the finish line.

Olivia whistled when Sofia exited the arena.

Sofia panted for breath as Kit Kat trotted past Julia, who was waiting for her turn. Julia tossed her hair, lifted her chin, and with a "humph" she led her appaloosa into the ring.

Julia urged her gelding on, yanking on his lead rope and shouting at him. But the more Julia pushed him, the slower her horse trotted. It looked as if she were trying to drag him through the course. Sofia suppressed a laugh. *Look who doesn't have control of her horse, now!*

A few minutes later, the announcer's voice vibrated through the speaker. Sofia could barely breathe as the competitors were called to receive their ribbons. Only three horses had jumped clean in the jump-off. The fastest would win the blue.

"In third place, Julia Blackstone-Hill..."

Perhaps it wasn't the best example of good sportsmanship, but Sofia couldn't help laughing and giving Ryan a playful punch in the ribs. Kit Kat had beaten Julia and Razz twice in a row.

Julia scowled and threw her ribbon on the ground.

"In second place, number 248, Emily Simpson, with Hocus Pocus."

Grace swung Sofia up into a hug as the others broke into applause. They'd done it!

"And winning the eight to twelve-year-old jumping class is number 117, Sofia Ruiz with Candy Ridge Truly Scrumptious."

Beaming, Sofia strode forward and claimed her prize. She kissed Kit Kat's nose before tucking the blue rosette into her halter.

"Woo hoo!" Ryan danced, waving his arms over his head. "I knew you'd win."

Sofia laughed. "I thought you were worried about the *rude girl.*"

Olivia grinned. "She didn't stand a chance against you and Kit Kat."

"We need a Mini Whinnies group photo." Pastor Amy reached for her phone. "Sofia and Kit Kat, and Ryan, and Olivia. And Grace, we need you, too."

"Don't forget Stephanie and Snickers." Sofia grabbed Stephanie's hand.

Grampy fumbled with his phone. "Uh, how do you get it to take a picture, again?"

"Oh, Grampy." Sofia rolled her eyes. *If only Mom had been here to see me win.*

***

Sofia reached under Snickers' belly to tighten the leather cinch on his harness. "Hey, Olivia, are you ready for your second blue ribbon of the day?"

"You'd better believe it." Olivia fastened the crupper around Snickers' tail. "Snickers and I are going to win both driving classes."

Grampy approached and motioned for Sofia to step away from the others. "I just called your mother."

Sofia's throat tightened. *She's not coming, is she?*

"You know they got stuck in some traffic coming out of Boston."

"Yeah, but they're going to be here soon, right?" How bad could the traffic be?

"Well," Grampy looked at the ground and paused before meeting Sofia's eyes. "After they got into Maine they stopped for something to eat." Grampy swallowed. "And since it was getting late they decided to do some sightseeing and meet you at the house instead of driving all the way up here."

Sofia fought back the hot tears forming at the corners of her eyes. "So, Mom's not bothering to show up."

With her classes now finished, Sofia supposed it didn't matter much anyway. Mom had already missed her victory in the jumping event. But she'd promised.

Grampy shook his head. "I'm sorry. If you want, I can take you home now so you can see her."

"No. Olivia still has her two driving events. I want to support her."

Because that's what you do when you care about people.

"I understand." Grampy reached his arm around Sofia's shoulders and drew her into his embrace.

She squeezed her eyes shut, imagining Mom giggling and flirting with Paul while *sightseeing.* Sofia had never met this man, but she realized with a sickening jolt that he must be more important to Mom than she was. Why else would Mom abandon her to spend the summer in England? Why else would Mom leave Boston hours after the horse show even began? Why else would she choose to *stop for lunch* when it meant missing Sofia's horse show? Sofia wondered if Mom had ever intended to make it to the show in the first place. Probably not.

"What's wrong?" Stephanie asked.

Sofia opened her eyes and wiped a hand across her cheeks.

"Sofia's mother isn't going to make it to the show," Grampy said.

Stephanie frowned, her brow furrowing and her eyes narrowing. "Why doesn't that surprise me?" she muttered under her breath.

Grampy sighed.

Stephanie covered Sofia's clenched fist with her hand. "You're a hard worker, extremely responsible, and kind to both your friends and your horses. The fact that your mother isn't here doesn't change any of that. She's a fool for not being here to see what a fine young woman you've become. I'd be proud to call you my daughter."

Sofia's eyes widened. Did Stephanie really mean that?

I wish Stephanie were my mother.

Sofia bit her lip. No, she couldn't think that way.

Chapter 28

Sofia stared out the window, barely noticing the passing landscape as the Murphy's van followed Stephanie's horse trailer. Ryan snored and Olivia stirred briefly before nestling her head on Sofia's shoulder again. Olivia's three blue ribbons rested on her lap.

In just a few minutes, Sofia would see Mom for the first time in two months. And she wasn't ready.

For weeks Sofia had rehearsed the speech that she hoped would convince Mom to let her return to Gramma Lisa's house. But was that what she truly wanted? She loved Gramma Lisa and desperately missed Sundance. But to move back to Connecticut would mean leaving Grampy and Olivia and Ryan. She would have to say goodbye to Snickers and Kit Kat, Grace and Stephanie, Pastor Amy and David and everyone at the Good Shepherd Community Church.

Pastor Amy turned toward the backseat. "Do you want us to drop you off at your Grampy's?"

"Maybe I should help with the horses first."

"I'm sure they'll be all set," said Pastor Amy. "Stephanie and Grace will understand."

Sofia hesitated. Pastor Amy was right, and she couldn't put off seeing Mom forever. "I guess you can drop me off. Thanks."

A few minutes later, they turned into Grampy's driveway. A fire-engine-red sports car was parked next to his beat-up Subaru.

"Whoa, is that a Mustang convertible?" Ryan asked.

"It is." David sounded impressed.

"Good luck," Olivia said as Sofia opened the door.

Sofia's hand shook slightly as she slid the van's door shut. She lingered in Grampy's driveway, watching the Murphy family drive away before trudging up the porch steps. She hovered in front of the door a moment longer. As she reached for the handle, it swung open.

"Honey Bear!" Mom screeched, pulling Sofia into a hug.

Sofia hugged back, feeling hot and self-conscious.

Mom stepped away and smiled. "You look so grown up. And what a darling shirt. I love it."

"It's for the horse show," Sofia muttered. *The one you didn't bother to see.*

"Yes, Grampy told me all about it, and how you pushed that handicapped girl in the wheelchair. You are such a kind, sweet girl," Mom said.

"Her name is Olivia. And she won all three of her classes."

"I'm sure you helped her a lot." Mom motioned to the man standing behind her. "I want you to meet Paul."

Paul extended his hand toward Sofia. "So nice to finally meet you. I've heard a lot about you."

Sofia had heard British accents before, but rarely in person. Mom's boyfriend sounded sophisticated. She could understand why Mom might like his voice. But she wasn't sure what else Mom would find attractive about him. Her other boyfriends had been muscular and tough looking. Paul was slightly built and pale, like he didn't work outside often. His large nose didn't fit his small, narrow face. Sofia could see deep wrinkles forming around his eyes, and with his gray, thinning hair, he looked much too old to be Mom's boyfriend.

"Your mother told me how much you love horses," Paul said.

Sofia nodded.

"We've got some great news to tell you, Honey Bear. And of course, we want to know all about your summer. Paul and I would like to take you out to a nice restaurant. We want to make it special."

"Uh..." Sofia looked at Grampy.

Grampy cleared his throat. "Mandi, I'd be happy to order some pizza. It's been a long day for all of you."

Mom wrinkled her nose. "Don't be silly. Paul's treating. We want it to be special. Just the three of us."

They weren't inviting Grampy? If this bothered him, Sofia couldn't tell.

Paul looked at Grampy, apparently without a hint of guilt over not including him in their plans. "Do you have any recommendations for a nice place?"

"Captain Bob's Boathouse," Sofia said. "Grace works there."

"You've been?" asked Mom.

"The Murphys took me. Olivia's parents."

"Is it a seafood restaurant?"

"Yes. They have the best seafood around."

"That sounds excellent," said Paul.

Sofia suppressed a grin. She couldn't wait to see the look on Mom's face when she and Paul were greeted by singing and dancing lobsters and that creepy animatronic fisherman. This would be special.

**

"Oh." Mom groaned as Paul maneuvered the fancy convertible into a parking space at Captian Bob's Boathouse. Seagulls swarmed overhead, and Sofia hoped the car would be covered in droppings by the time they left.

"At least the parking lot's full. Maybe it's a diamond in the rough," Paul said.

The lobby was packed with people waiting for a table. If anything, it looked shabbier than it had in June, after a busy summer packed with tourists. Sofia pointed to the plastic lobsters. "They're so funny. Wait 'til the music comes on."

Mom flinched when the wailing electric guitars and drums activated the three lobsters.

Sofia giggled as they stood up on their tails and snapped their claws. "See, that one's missing a claw."

Mom winced and looked at Paul.

"Welcome to Bob's Boathouse," the robotic fisherman proclaimed from his wooden barrel. His fishing rod waved up and down feebly.

Sofia laughed.

"This is quite the place." Paul wrapped his arm around Mom and murmured something in her ear.

A woman dressed in a sailor outfit directed them to a booth and handed them menus.

Paul opened his menu. "I see they have fish 'n chips. Making us Brits feel welcome."

"And they have lobster." Mom reached across the booth and brushed a stray curl from Sofia's forehead. "You can't spend the summer in Maine without eating a lobster."

The curl fell back into place as Sofia shook her head. "I'm going to have Bob's Bucket 'O Clams. It's a giant bucket overflowing with fried clams and French fries. I'll never be able to eat it all, but I can throw the leftovers to the seagulls." *That should annoy Mom.*

Sofia's eyes widened as Grace approached their booth. "I didn't know you were working tonight."

"Neither did I. They were short-handed and called me in," Grace said. "But what a wonderful surprise! You brought your mother and her friend from England."

Paul and Mom introduced themselves, and Grace took their orders. She returned with their drinks a few minutes later.

"You should be very proud of Sofia. She's a fine horsewoman." Grace handed Sofia her chocolate milk. "I'm sorry you missed the show."

"Oh, I know. So much traffic," Mom said.

Sofia balled her fists under the table.

Grace nodded without her usual smile and retreated to the kitchen.

Mom leaned her head on Paul's shoulder and touched his hand. Their fingers intertwined. "Honey Bear. I'm so excited, I can't keep it quiet anymore." She giggled. "Paul and I are getting married!"

Sofia stared, mouth slightly open. "You're getting... married?" Her stomach clenched.

Paul reached his free arm across the booth to grasp Sofia's hand. "I love your mother, Sofia. And I'm so pleased to be gaining such a beautiful daughter."

Sofia yanked her hand away. *You're not my father.*

Mom sniffed and dabbed her eyes. "Sofia, I know it's been hard for you the last few years since your father abandoned us. But Paul's a wonderful man. He'll take care of us. We'll be a happy family."

Sofia's throat tightened as she swallowed back the words she wished she had the courage to say.

Mom had never married before. When Sofia had asked her why she hadn't married her dad, she just shook her head and said that he wasn't the marrying type, whatever that meant. A few months after he'd left, there'd been a guy who rode a motorcycle. What was his name? Rick, maybe? Then there'd been Tom, an enormous man covered with tattoos, but they'd broken up after a year. It was just as well, because he scared Sofia. And now there was Paul, a total stranger proclaiming his joy in gaining Sofia as a daughter.

After an uncomfortably long silence, Mom said, "Honey Bear, I've picked out the perfect wedding dress. Do you want to see it?" She fiddled with her phone and slid it across the booth to Sofia.

"It's nice," Sofia mumbled, without really looking at it.

"I want you to be the flower girl." Mom took the phone back and selected another photo. "You will be the prettiest girl there."

I'm eleven years old, Mom. Who ever heard of an eleven-year old flower girl?

"I can't wait for you to meet your new sisters and brother," Paul said.

Sofia looked up. Sisters and a brother? Sofia had often dreamed of having siblings. What would these children be like? Would they want to be friends with her? Would they fight like Olivia did with Ryan? So many questions swirled around her mind.

"Do they live with you?"

Paul chuckled. "Oh, no. They're on their own, now. My youngest, James, graduated from Cambridge last year. He's twenty-three. Rebecca is twenty-seven. And Hannah will turn thirty next month. I can hardly believe it."

Thirty years old! Hannah was almost as old as Sofia's mother, which would mean Paul must be old enough to be a grandfather. No wonder he had so many wrinkles and gray hair. Why did Mom want to marry this guy?

Mom didn't appear to notice Sofia's discomfort, or perhaps she did, and chose to ignore it. Sofia wasn't sure.

"When are you getting married?" Maybe they'd get into a huge fight and break up before it was too late.

Mom patted Paul's hand. "We decided that it's best to wait until Christmas. That will give you time to settle into your new life before the big day."

What new life?

And then it hit her with such force that she almost bolted from the table. "We're moving to England?"

Chapter 29

In all her agonized plans about her future, Sofia had never considered the possibility that Mom would get married and expect her to move to England. Her face burned.

Mom's smile faltered. "Well, yes, honey. Paul has a beautiful home there. And Paul wants you to attend Marlston House in September."

"Is that a school or something?"

Paul nodded. "I know that your education so far has been a bit...lacking. But it's not too late to redirect your path. Marlston House is an excellent school. They will help you get back on track."

Sofia's jaw clenched. It wasn't her fault that Mom had yanked her out of fifth grade before she could finish the year.

"My daughters attended Roedean, which in my opinion is the finest girls' school in the United Kingdom. They passed their entrance exams at your age. But don't worry, with hard work I'm sure you'll be accepted to Roedean soon enough. And since you have turned eleven, you will be old enough to be a boarding student at Marlston House."

"What is a boarding student?" That didn't sound good.

"It means you will live there, at the school. You will live in a house with other girls your age," said Paul.

"You want me to move to another country and stay at a boarding school?" Sofia's voice trembled. "I wouldn't even be living with you?"

"Honey Bear, it's an incredible opportunity for you."

"Marlston House is an excellent school, Sofia. They'll prepare you for the entrance exam. Then you can be accepted to Roedean, where you will be educated by the very best teachers in the world. They will mold your character and challenge you to accomplish things you never dreamed you could do. And when you finish, you will be able to get into a top university, hopefully Cambridge or Oxford."

Sofia clenched her fists under the table. What right did Paul have to plan out her entire life? And Mom was going right along with it.

Mom shifted, looking uncomfortable. "Paul is being very generous. It costs a lot of money to go there."

"Mandi, don't tell her that," Paul chided. "The important thing is that you will have a top-notch education, just like I gave my own children. They're very successful, accomplished people. And you will be, too."

Sofia no longer cared about holding back her words. "You're planning to ship me off for other people to watch over me, just like you always do! That way, you can do what you want without having to think about me. That's not what I think of when I think of a happy family." She slammed her fist on the table, sending her fork skittering off the edge and onto the floor. People at the nearby booths turned and stared at her.

"Please..." Mom hissed.

At that moment, Grace appeared at their table with a tray of food. She smiled, but Sofia noticed that it wasn't Grace's usual grin. "I hope you enjoy your meal. Would you like a refill on your chocolate milk, Sofia?"

Sofia nodded. Her hot flash of anger was rapidly dissolving into icy resignation. Mom was getting married to Paul, and she'd be dragged off to a boarding school in England. She'd never see Sundance again. Unless...

"Why can't I live with Gramma Lisa?"

"This isn't the right time to discuss your grandmother, Sofia." Mom glanced toward Grace, who was already half-way across the large dining room.

Sofia folded her arms and glared at Mom. "You can move to England, but let me live with Gramma Lisa."

"This isn't a good time—"

"I don't care!" Sofia shouted.

Mom's nostrils flared. "You can't live there."

"Why not? Just because you had a stupid fight with her?"

"You're not safe there." Mom's face flushed.

"That's not true." Sofia couldn't prevent her voice from rising again. "Gramma Lisa loves me. She would never hurt me. She's not like you."

"Sofia!" Paul snapped. "Do not talk to your mother that way."

"Please, Paul," Mom said. "Let me—"

"No. She needs to learn respect." Paul fixed his eyes on Sofia. "Is that what you think? That your mother is hurting you? She's been protecting you."

Sofia returned his glare. "I don't need protecting."

"Clearly you do. But you're too wrapped up in yourself to see it."

"Paul – "

"No, Mandi. Sofia seems to have it in her head that she knows better than her own mother." Paul's eyes bore into Sofia. "Your mother didn't want to hurt you with the truth. But I will. Lisa's piece of trash boyfriend is a monster who abuses little girls. And if your mother didn't intervene, you would have been his next victim."

"He's not..." Sofia's voice faltered. "He never..." But her stomach lurched as she remembered Mike's unwelcome compliments. The uncomfortable hugs. The way his eyes wandered over her body when she rode Sundance.

Mom reached her hand across the table, but Sofia snatched it away. "Honey Bear, Mike spent time in prison for –"

"No!" Sofia leapt from the booth, scattering her uneaten fried clams. "I... I...think I'm going to throw up..." She covered her mouth with her hands and bolted for the bathroom.

Sofia raced through the door marked "Gulls", startling an elderly woman who was washing her hands at the bathroom sink. Sofia's stomach heaved as she frantically locked the stall door, but she managed to hold back retching until she reached the toilet.

"Oh, dear," muttered the woman.

Sofia moaned and vomited a second time.

"I'll get help," the lady said.

"No, I don't need – " Sofia's stomach contracted and she was sick a third time.

It couldn't be true. Gramma Lisa loved Sofia. She would never let Mike hurt her. Except...

"Sofia," Mom called. "Sofia, are you okay?"

"Go away. I don't want to talk to you."

"Don't be silly." Mom rattled the stall door. "Sofia, open the door."

"No." Sofia grabbed a handful of toilet paper and wiped her face. She nearly vomited a fourth time before quickly flushing the previous contents of her stomach down the drain.

She heard the bathroom door bang shut, followed by Grace's voice. "Sofia? I heard you were sick."

Sofia stifled a sob. "Yeah."

"Honey Bear, please open the door," Mom pleaded.

She couldn't face Mom, not now. She couldn't bear to know the details about how Gramma Lisa's boyfriend went to prison for something horrible. She didn't want to hear Mom tell her how irresponsible Gramma Lisa had been to let a monster like that into her life, or what might have happened if Mom hadn't taken her away that night.

Mom knocked again. "Paul and I need to take you back to Grampy's."

Sofia didn't want to drive home in Paul's fancy car and listen to more of his plans for her future. Who was he to jump into her life like that and tell her what to do? He wasn't her father. He wasn't even her stepfather yet. She never wanted to see Paul again.

"I want Grace to take me home." Sofia's throat felt raw and her voice sounded scratchy.

"You're being ridiculous," Mom said. "Stop making a scene and open the door."

"Leave me alone."

Mom exhaled loudly.

Sofia began to cry. She wished she were in her room, hiding under the blankets. But it wasn't her room, was it? It was Grampy's guest room, and soon it would be empty. There'd be some other bed waiting for her at a boarding school in England.

Grace spoke from the other side of the stall door. "Mandi, Sofia's had a really long, emotional day. She's been up since before dawn and I'm sure she's completely exhausted. It's not really my business, but – "

"No, it isn't your business. Don't you have tables to wait on?" Mom growled.

"I'll take you home, Sofia," Grace said, her voice high and tense.

"You have no right—"

"Mom, please let me go with her." Sofia's hand hovered over the lock.

"Fine." Mom sniffed. "Though Paul isn't going to like this one bit."

***

Sofia trembled in the passenger seat as Grace drove her home. Mom hadn't made a scene in the restaurant, but Sofia suspected she would be less likely to hold back in front of Grampy. It was only a matter of time before Mom and Paul would bang her bedroom door, demanding to speak with her.

"Do you want to talk about it?" Grace asked.

Sofia stared out the window at the passing trees.

"It's okay if you don't," Grace said.

Sofia closed her eyes and sighed. She didn't want to talk. She didn't want to think.

They drove in silence until Grace turned into Grampy's driveway.

"You've got my number. Call or text me any time. I don't care how late it is." Grace touched Sofia's hand. "I love you. Don't you forget it."

"Love you, too." Sofia collapsed into Grace's arms and sobbed.

Chapter 30

Sofia awoke to the buzzing of her six o'clock alarm. Time to help feed Snickers and Kit Kat. Her face felt puffy and her eyelids had crusted shut. She rubbed her nose and squinted at the early morning light creeping under her curtains.

There'd been no late-night knock on the door. Mom hadn't come.

For a moment she dared to believe that the previous night had been a terrible dream. Mom wasn't really getting married to Paul. She wouldn't be moving to England and attending a boarding school for girls. And Gramma Lisa's boyfriend wasn't an evil monster who had spent time in prison for hurting children.

Sofia tossed off the covers, stretched, and stepped onto the floor. Someone had neatly arranged her horse show ribbons on top of the dresser. Grampy was right. The pink rosette was kind of pretty. She picked up the blue ribbon she'd won in the jumping class and flipped it over. Under the date and event, Olivia had scrawled *"Sofia 'n Kit Kat rule."*

She placed the ribbon next to the others before opening the top drawer of her dresser. She pulled out a clean shirt, shorts, and underwear and dressed quickly. Sofia tried to run her fingers through her hair, but her dark curls had knotted so completely that she gave up and reached for a Boston Red Sox cap Grampy had given to her. The horses wouldn't care how she looked as long as she fed them, and she'd have plenty of time to get ready for church after completing her barn chores.

After a brief stop in the bathroom, Sofia entered the kitchen, hoping that Grampy still had a few strawberry Pop-Tarts in the cupboard. Her stomach rumbled, and she remembered that she hadn't eaten her fried clams last night.

She rummaged through a cardboard box and found a single remaining Pop-Tart. She unwrapped the pastry from its silver foil and slid it into the toaster.

Sofia glanced into the living room and froze. Mom was asleep on the couch. Her long blonde hair hung in tangles over her shoulders and mouth. She wore the same blouse and pants from the night before. Several crumpled tissues lay on the floor.

Where was Paul? Sofia tip-toed past Mom and stared out the window. The red Mustang wasn't there.

The toaster binged, and Mom's eyes flew open. "Sofia?"

Sofia's heart raced. "Yeah?"

Mom sat up, brushing the hair from her face. "Honey Bear, I'm so sorry."

Maybe Mom expected her to say that it was alright, but it wasn't. Sofia crossed her arms and stared at her.

"Paul shouldn't have told you about Mike. I didn't want to hurt you."

Sofia narrowed her eyes. "You kept that a secret because you *didn't want to hurt me*?"

"I thought it was better that way." Mom stood and stepped toward Sofia, her arms outstretched.

Sofia shook her head and backed away. "I had a life there, Mom. Gramma Lisa. My friends. My horse! What did you think? That I'd magically forget about them? Well, I've got some news for you, Mom. It didn't work."

Mom's face flushed. "I guess that wasn't fair to you."

"No. It wasn't." Sofia felt her face growing hot, too. "And if Gramma Lisa's boyfriend was really such a bad man, why didn't you ask if he did anything to me?"

Mom looked at the floor. "He didn't... Please tell me he didn't hurt you."

"He..." Hot bile burned Sofia's throat. "He made me feel...I don't know. He was creepy."

"Oh, Honey Bear, I was so worried he might have done something to you." Mom jumped from the couch and rushed forward, reaching her arms around Sofia. "Gramma Lisa is so irresponsible."

Sofia tore away from Mom's embrace. "Don't blame her!"

Mom's lips tightened. "When I heard Mum was dating Mike, I looked him up online. That's when I discovered he's a monster."

Sofia wished she could flee to her room, and hide under her covers. But she had to know the truth. "Did Gramma Lisa know that Mike was a...bad person?"

"She's *says* she didn't." Mom spat the words. "She told me she would break up with him right away. But she put you in danger, Sofia. I needed to protect you."

So Gramma Lisa hadn't known about Mike's past, and she'd promised to break up with him for Sofia's sake. Why did Mom force Sofia to move? It had all been for nothing! Anger pulsed through her. "If you wanted to keep me safe, why did you leave me again? Oh, yeah. 'Cause of Paul."

Mom raised her hands, her eyes wide. "Sofia, please. I did it for you."

"For me? You don't do things for me. You do things for you."

Mom looked as if Sofia had punched her in the stomach. "That's not true. I want the best for you. You don't know how hard it is, sometimes. I don't have any money or a place we can call our own. I can't give you the kind of life you deserve. But that's changed now. Paul will take care of us."

"I don't need Paul to take care of me," Sofia said, her voice hard. "I've been taking care of myself just fine without him. And without you."

"Honey Bear, you don't realize what Paul wants to give you. I met his kids, and they're just like him, smart and rich and successful. Paul's willing to help you get ahead in life. He'll give you the opportunities I never got when I was your age. You can grow up to be something."

"I don't want him to control my life!"

"He just wants to help you. He's a good man."

Mom looked as if she were on the verge of tears. Sofia wanted to rage at her, to punish her for abandoning her, to exact revenge. But Mom seemed so vulnerable, so sad. So...lonely. Sofia swallowed. How could she get Mom to listen?

"Mom, I don't want to go to a boarding school. And I don't want to move to England."

Mom frowned. "But Paul and I are getting married. He'll be your stepfather. We're going to be a family."

"We're already a family." Sofia didn't want to live with Paul. But if Mom really loved him... She took a deep breath and exhaled slowly. "We could all live here with Grampy."

Mom squeezed Sofia's hand. "Grampy was kind to let you live here for the summer. We can't ask him for more than that."

"Why not?"

"Oh, Honey Bear. Grampy loves you, and I'm sure he'd do his best. But he's an old man. It would be too much for him."

"Then we can get our own house. Near Grampy. I can go to school with Olivia and Ryan. I can go to the barn everyday to take care of Snickers and Kit Kat. And maybe...maybe Gramma Lisa would let me bring Sundance here."

Mom sniffed. "Honey Bear, Paul's family and his businesses are in England. He won't leave and move here."

Sofia stiffened and stepped back. "Well, my family and friends are here. And I'm not moving to England, so I guess you'll have to choose if you want to live with Paul or me."

"You don't get to decide these things."

"Then you decide. Paul or me?"

"You're not being fair."

"I have to go. I've got horses to feed." Sofia stomped to the door.

"Wait!"

Sofia slammed the door and stumbled across Grampy's driveway to the shed that housed her bike. The look on Mom's face had told her all she needed to know. Mom would choose Paul. Mom had known this guy for three months, and already he was more important than her own daughter.

Sofia blinked and rubbed her eyes as she struggled to see the path in front of her. Her bike wobbled as she rode over a patch of loose gravel. *Mom doesn't love me.*

Did Grampy? Maybe he was looking forward to the end of the summer when he wouldn't have the responsibility of caring for her anymore.

Nobody wanted her.

Chapter 31

Stephanie was leading Kit Kat into the mini's paddock when Sofia dismounted her bicycle. "Good morning, Sofia. I didn't expect to see you."

Sofia attempted to smile, but it felt more like a wince. Grace must have told Stephanie all about last night's disaster at the restaurant. Otherwise, Stephanie would have scolded her for being late to feed the horses.

Stephanie closed the gate, carefully locking it shut. "I haven't finished all the chores yet. Did you want to muck out the stalls?"

Sofia nodded, grateful not to have to answer questions about Mom or Paul or her future.

She entered the barn, removed the pitchfork from its hook on the wall and positioned the empty wheelbarrow beside the entrance to Snickers' empty stall. She scooped a pile of manure, sifted out the clean wood shavings, and plopped the rest into the wheelbarrow with a loud *thunk*. Snickers always pooped in the same area along the back wall of his stall. *Thunk. Thunk.* And his pee spot could be found towards the middle and a little over to the left. Sofia removed a patch of soggy, discolored shavings, ammonia filling her nostrils.

That was the thing about horses. Life could be spinning out of control, the ground could threaten to swallow you up, and your horse would still pee and poop in the same spot every day.

Stephanie appeared at the barn door, cradling two steaming mugs. "I made some hot chocolate, if you want some."

Sofia dragged her arm across her wet cheeks. "Okay." She sniffed and leaned the pitchfork against Kit Kat's stall door.

Stephanie handed her the mug and Sofia followed her outside.

They sat at the picnic table, watching the horses and sipping their cocoa in silence. Snickers flattened his ears as Kit Kat attempted to snatch a bite of his hay. Chastened, the mare wandered over to her ration. A minute later, Snickers pushed Kit Kat from her hay bag, claiming it for himself. Kit Kat circled back to munch on Snickers' hay.

"Snickerdoodles is such a brat sometimes," Stephanie said. "But you did a great job with him at the show yesterday."

"Thanks." Sofia blinked back a fresh batch of tears.

Stephanie placed her mug on the table. "Grace tells me that your mother is engaged."

Sofia sighed. "Yeah."

"That's going to be a big change for you, I expect."

Sofia swallowed the lump forming in her throat. "They want me to go to a boarding school in England."

"Oh?" Stephanie picked up her mug and swirled the hot liquid before taking another sip. "What do you think of that idea?"

"I hate it."

"Hmm."

"You think I should go?" Sofia asked, unsure how to interpret Stephanie's response.

"It doesn't matter what I think you should do. The question is what do you want?"

Sofia stared at her lap. "What I want isn't going to happen."

"Maybe not," Stephanie said. "Life doesn't always give us what we want. Still, I'd like to hear your thoughts, if you want to share them."

"I don't want to move to England." Sofia poked at the dregs of chocolate coating the bottom of her mug. "For a long time I thought I wanted to move back in with my Gramma Lisa. But I can't because of something that happened. It's a long story."

She expected Stephanie to ask her to explain, but she simply folded her hands under her chin.

Sofia watched a squirrel scamper along the top rail of the paddock fence before scurrying up a pine tree. "I finally realized that what I really want is to live with Grampy, and go to school with Olivia and Ryan.

I'd like to see you and Grace and the horses every day. And I wish Mom would stay here with me instead of going to England."

"I can understand that."

"But it's not going to happen, because Mom's getting married. And Paul doesn't want to live here."

Stephanie nodded. "And you don't think she'll let you stay here with Grampy?"

Sofia took a shaky breath. "Mom and I kind of got into a fight about it."

"What about your horse? I know you miss him terribly." Stephanie took another sip of her hot chocolate. "Do you think your grandmother would allow you to keep him somewhere else?"

Will Stephanie let me keep Sundance here?

"I've never asked her. Would you..." Sofia didn't dare to finish her question.

Stephanie smiled and nodded vigorously.

Sofia's heart pounded. Was Stephanie really offering to take care of Sundance? "If I can convince Mom to let me stay here with Grampy, could Sundance live here? With you?"

"That depends." Stephanie grinned. "Will you muck out his stall every day?"

"Yes."

"And will you continue to help with feeding and the other barn chores?"

"Yes!"

"Will you help me clean up the pasture and repair the fence? The paddock isn't big enough for him, and I wouldn't want him to get into trouble with the minis."

"Yes!" Sofia jumped from the table and wrapped her arms around Stephanie's shoulders.

"Of course, you shouldn't get ahead of yourself, Sofia. You're going to have to work all of it out with your family. What does your Grampy think about you living with him?"

"I don't know."

"Maybe you should ask him."

Sofia released Stephanie from her embrace. "Can I go right now?"

Stephanie laughed. "I'm sure Grace won't mind finishing up the chores."

Sofia raced back to Grampy's house. Sundance could live with Stephanie and Grace! All she had to do was convince Mom. She didn't know how, but she'd have to find a way. She pounded up the steps and leapt through the door.

Grampy looked up from his newspaper, his brow furrowed. "What's wrong?"

Her eyes darted around the kitchen. "Where's Mom?"

Grampy put down the paper and stood, frowning. "Paul picked her up about five minutes ago."

Sofia froze. "She's... gone?"

How could Mom leave without saying goodbye? She never should have argued with her, never should have forced Mom to choose between her and Paul. "Is she coming back?"

Grampy placed his hand on Sofia's arm. "I don't know what she's doing. She seemed quite upset."

"It's my fault. I drove her away." Sofia collapsed onto a kitchen chair and sobbed.

Grampy settled back into his chair, reached across the table, and clasped Sofia's hand. "Oh, sweetie. It's not your fault."

"They're getting married. They want me to move to England and go to a boarding school."

The wrinkles around Grampy's mouth deepened. "Your mother told me last night."

"I told her I don't want to go." Sofia's shoulders trembled. "I said she had to choose. Me or Paul. And now she's gone."

Grampy shook his head. "Your mother loves you. She probably left so she could talk with Paul. I'm sure she has a lot of complicated feelings."

I have a lot of complicated feelings, too.

Sofia stared at the veins criss-crossing Grampy's gnarled hand. "I want to live here. With you."

Grampy squeezed Sofia's hand. "I want you to live with me, too."

"Really?"

"Really."

"It wouldn't be too much?" Sofia dabbed her cheeks.

"What on earth do you mean?"

"Mom said it was too much to ask you because you're old."

"I'm not *that* old." Grampy's mustache twitched. "And think of all the chores you can do to help me in my feeble state. You can mow the lawn and vacuum the floor and clean the bathroom and—"

"Oh, Grampy!" Sofia ran around the table and threw her arms around him. "I love you so much."

Chapter 32

Pastor Amy was finishing the announcements when Sofia and Grampy slid into the pew behind Mrs. Smith and Mrs. Weaver. Olivia waved from the opposite side of the church and motioned for Sofia to join her.

Sofia shrugged and shook her head. She usually sat with Olivia and Ryan, but she couldn't bear the thought of answering their questions. Not that she *could* answer them.

Grampy opened the bulletin and pointed to the line of text the congregation was reading in unison. Sofia stared at it without seeing, her eyes scratchy and tired.

"Amen," the congregation said.

She stood with the other members of the church as they began to sing. One of the younger boys beat out a rhythm as he slapped a hand drum. Others clapped in time with the music. The sound washed over Sofia's numb mind, and her lips moved without awareness of the words forming there.

The music changed to a slower and sweeter tune.

> *Amazing Grace, how sweet the sound,*
> *that saved a wretch like me.*

Sofia didn't notice Mom until she rested her hand on Sofia's shoulder. Her hair was no longer tangled, and she had changed her outfit, but there were dark shadows under her eyes. Sofia looked behind her for Paul, but he wasn't with her.

Mom's high, tremulous voice joined Grampy's and the others.

> *I once was lost, but now am found,*
> *was blind but now I see.*

Grampy's hand brushed Sofia's back. She looked into his lined face. His eyes glistened. "I love you," he silently mouthed.

A spark of hope flared within Sofia's raw heart, smoldering, burning. Mom was here. She hadn't chosen Paul over her. Not yet, at least.

She reached for Mom's hand and squeezed, willing her to understand. *Stay with me, Mom.*

The hymn ended and the congregation sat.

Pastor Amy asked, "Does anyone want to share something they're thankful for?"

Olivia's hand shot into the air, just as it had so many times during Mini Whinnies meetings. She stood and faced the members of the church. "I went to a horse show yesterday with Ryan and Sofia. And I won all three of my events."

Several people clapped.

"One of the events is called hunter, and you have to lead the horse over jumps. I couldn't have done it by myself, so Sofia helped me. We practiced a lot before the show, and Sofia and I made a great team. Even though I got to take home a blue ribbon, she deserved it just as much as I did. So I thank God for my best friend, Sofia."

Sofia remembered Olivia's confession on the night she'd slept over at the Murphy's house. Olivia thought her leg braces and crutches made others feel uncomfortable. She believed it didn't matter that she was the smartest kid in her class. How could anyone treat this talented, generous, brash, *fierce* girl like she was invisible?

You're my best friend, too.

Mom leaned into Sofia and whispered, "I'm proud of you, Honey Bear."

Mrs. Weaver grabbed the front of the pew and rose unsteadily. "I'm thankful that my grandson came to visit me yesterday."

A middle-aged woman who Sofia didn't recognize said, "Thank you all for praying for me. The doctors were able to remove the tumor, and the test results show I'm cancer free."

The congregation broke into applause.

Pastor Amy asked, "Is there anyone else who has something they'd like to share?"

Mom's hand trembled under Sofia's. Mom looked at her, her cheeks pink and her eyes watery. Then she leaned forward and stood.

"I'm thankful for my daughter." Her voice quavered. "And for my grandfather."

Mom sniffed loudly and returned to her seat. "I've made a real mess of things, and...I don't know what to do." She covered her face and wept.

"Oh, Mom," Sofia said. "Please don't leave me again."

"I won't, Honey Bear. I won't."

She's not going to leave me. Did this mean Mom would agree to live with her at Grampy's? That Sundance would join them? It was the longest church service Sofia ever sat through. When Pastor Amy offered the final prayer, Sofia stood, grabbed Mom's hand, and pulled her into the aisle. She had to know Mom's plans.

Instead they were bombarded by Grampy's friends. Mrs. Weaver hugged Mom, and Mrs. Smith told her that they would be praying for her. An ancient man shuffled over, wishing them well with a raspy voice. Pastor Amy reached for Sofia, pulling her into a bone-crushing embrace.

"Excuse me." Olivia waved one of her crutches to push away the crowd. "Let me through, people."

Ryan followed in her wake.

"Sofia's Mom." Olivia looked from Mom to Sofia and back again. "Nice to finally meet you."

"You can call me Mandi."

Olivia grinned. "Hi, Mandi. I know exactly what you should do."

Pastor Amy frowned and shook her head at her daughter.

Olivia rolled her eyes. "I heard her tell Sofia she didn't know what to do. I'm just helping her out."

Ryan tugged at his twin's arm, but she didn't budge.

"I think you need to let them figure that out for themselves, Olivia," Pastor Amy said firmly.

Sofia urged Grampy and Mom out the church building, desperate to know what Mom was thinking. They couldn't talk in front of all these people. As they stepped into the parking lot, Sofia froze. "What is he doing here?"

Paul leaned against the door of his red Mustang convertible, surrounded by a circle of admirers. David caressed the gleaming hood while another man peered inside the leather interior.

"For goodness sake, it's only a rental car," Grampy muttered.

Paul straightened as Sofia and Mom approached. His smile didn't reach his cold, hard eyes. "Mandi." He glanced at his watch.

Sofia laced her fingers through Mom's shaking hand. "Please Mom, don't let him take you away from me."

"Excuse me." Paul flicked his arm to dismiss the car enthusiasts. "I need to speak with my fiancée."

The men scattered but Grampy remained by Mom's side.

"Bill." Paul extended his hand to Grampy. "I'd like to have a word with Mandi and Sofia, please."

Grampy didn't move.

Paul cleared his throat.

Grampy put his arm around Sofia.

Paul glared at him and turned to Mom. "You told me you'd come right out with Sofia. I've been waiting here for nearly an hour."

"I'm sorry." Mom stared at the ground.

"Well, get in the car. It's a three hour drive to Bar Harbor. Does Sofia have her things packed?"

Sofia flinched at the sound of her name. What was Bar Harbor? Maybe Paul was punishing her for not wanting to attend boarding school in England. He was going to send her to some place even worse. Away from Grampy and Mom and Sundance.

"We're not going," Mom said.

"What?" Paul's nostrils flared. "Do you know how hard it was for me to reserve a suite at a decent hotel during the height of tourist season? We decided that we needed some time to together as a family, so Sofia could get to know me before we fly back home."

"Sofia doesn't want to go to school in England. She wants to live here," Mom said.

Paul folded his arms and looked at Sofia. It felt as if his narrowed eyes were injecting ice directly into her veins. She shivered and retreated into Grampy's arms.

"Sofia is a child." Paul scowled. "And we are her parents. It doesn't matter what she wants. We know what is best for her. She's going to – "

"You're not my parent," Sofia mumbled.

"I am your stepfather, young lady."

"Actually, Paul, you aren't her stepfather," Grampy said. "Not yet anyway."

"This is ridiculous. Get in the car, Mandi." Paul flung open the passenger's side door. "You, too, Sofia."

Mom shook her head. "Sofia is staying here, with Grampy. And I'm..."

Paul slammed the door. "You're what, Mandi?"

"I'm staying with her."

Chapter 33

It took Sofia six full days to prepare for Sundance's arrival. She helped Grace mow the overgrown grass and weeds and repair the loose fence boards. After Stephanie warned that horses can colic from eating fermenting grass, Sofia and Ryan competed to see who could scoop up the biggest heaps of clippings and remove them from Sundance's pasture. Olivia helped her move the miniature horses' tack, harness, and cart from Toby's old stall into the newly-remodeled feed room. Stephanie's neighbor delivered second-cut hay from his field and Sofia and Grace stacked the bales neatly into the hay loft.

Sofia's muscles ached, but she didn't complain.

She pulled her phone from her jeans pocket. Gramma Lisa was twenty minutes late. She wandered into the barn and checked the water bucket in Sundance's new stall. Yes, it was full. The fresh bedding was perfectly fluffed.

"Sofia! Sofia!" Ryan burst through the door. "They're coming down the driveway."

Sofia hurtled out of the stall. Her heart pounded.

A familiar green pick-up truck and horse trailer crunched over the gravel, stopping in front of the barn. The truck's door swung open and a short woman with bushy, graying hair stepped out.

"Gramma Lisa!" Sofia launched herself into her grandmother's arms. She smelled just as Sofia remembered, a mixture of horses and hay and lavender shampoo.

"I missed you so much, and so did Sundance," Gramma Lisa said. "He hollered the whole way up from Connecticut, but he's going to be so happy to see you."

A loud bang shook the trailer. It was followed by an ear-splitting neigh.

"Can we unload him now?" Sofia asked.

"You've got his stall ready?" Gramma Lisa asked. "We'll want to give him a bit of time to get used to his new surroundings. He's going to be nervous at first, and we don't want him running around or getting hurt."

Sofia nodded. "Stephanie warned me about that. And I didn't put any hay in his stall, because she told me you'd be bringing a few bales so he can get used to his new food slowly."

"That's right. We don't want him getting a belly-ache."

Olivia tapped one of her crutches on Sofia's foot. "Hey, are you going to introduce your grandmother to us, or what?"

Gramma Lisa cocked her head. "Hello. Are you Sofia's friend?"

"Yup. I'm her *best* friend, Olivia." She held out her hand. "And this is my brother, Ryan. And my mother, Amy. And Stephanie and Grace. And..." she turned back to look at Grampy and Mom. "I guess you already know them."

Gramma Lisa nodded curtly to Mom, who leaned onto the picnic table, her arms folded. Grampy looked from Mom to Gramma Lisa, as if unsure of what to say.

Sundance's explosive neighing reverberated through the trailer. Kit Kat answered him with a high whinny. Snickers snorted and tossed his mane. Sofia hoped Mom's tiff with Gramma Lisa wouldn't interfere with unloading Sundance. Her horse was getting more upset by the minute.

Stephanie stepped forward. "Ryan, could you grab a bale of hay off the back of Lisa's truck and bring it to the barn? Olivia, you can put a couple of flakes into Sundance's hay rack. Let's get this guy out of the trailer."

"I'll get his lead rope." Sofia's body jittered with anticipation. She was about to see her horse for the first time in months. Would he remember her?

Sofia dashed to the barn, returning with a brand new, purple lead rope decorated with red hearts.

"Maybe I should do it," Gramma Lisa said. "He's a bit worked up."

Stephanie put her hands on her hips. "Sofia can handle him."

"Hmm..." Gramma Lisa rubbed the back of her neck. "I guess there's plenty of us here to help if she needs it."

Hands shaking slightly, Sofia approached the side door of the trailer. She grasped the metal handle, pushed it down, and the door slid open.

And there was Sundance, his brown eyes wide and nostrils flared. He stretched his head through the opening of the door, reaching for Sofia, touching her hand with his soft nose.

She stepped into the trailer and ran her hands down her horse's golden neck. She brushed his white forelock from his eyes.

Sundance nickered, a low rumbling sound.

"I missed you, too, buddy."

Sofia fastened the lead to the noseband of Sundance's halter and unclipped the trailer tie. "Ready to move into your new home? You're going to love it here. And I'm going to see you every day."

Sundance nuzzled Sofia.

"Sofia, I'm letting down the ramp," Gramma Lisa called.

The rear wall of the trailer creaked as Gramma Lisa and Stephanie eased it to the ground. Gramma Lisa stepped onto the ramp and released the metal bar behind Sundance's rump.

Sundance began to rush backward, but Sofia steadied him. "One step at a time, buddy."

And then they were off the trailer, Sundance blinking in the sunshine.

"He's gorgeous," Olivia said. "I can't wait to ride him."

"Me, too," said Ryan.

Sofia grinned. "You're not afraid to ride a big horse?"

Ryan shook his head. "I can't wait!"

Grace gave Ryan a high-five. "Put my name on the list, too. I want a chance before I have to leave for college."

Stephanie wagged her finger at Grace and Ryan. "Don't forget this is Sofia's horse. And give that poor guy a few days to settle in before you start making plans."

Sofia smiled. She didn't mind sharing. And it would be fun to teach Ryan how to ride.

She led Sundance up and down the driveway, giving him a chance to stretch his legs after the long trailer ride. His ears pricked forward, taking in his new surroundings. He called out to Kit Kat and Snickers as they trotted along the fence line.

Stephanie and Gramma Lisa stood beside the trailer, deep in conversation. Sofia had agreed to take responsibility for Sundance's daily care and chores, but she had no means to pay for his upkeep. Gramma Lisa had promised to fund Sundance's vet and farrier bills. Now that Mom had ended her engagement to Paul, she was broke. Grampy offered to pay for Sundance's hay and grain rations until Mom got a job and was able to help out. Sofia wondered how long that might be. *Maybe I can earn some money mowing lawns and raking leaves for Grampy's friends from church.*

"We've got the hay ready for him," Olivia shouted from the barn.

Sofia stroked Sundance's muscular neck. "I'll be there in a minute."

She led her horse to Gramma Lisa, her eyes filling with tears. "Thank you."

Gramma Lisa rubbed Sundance's nose. "I'm going to miss this guy. But not as much as I miss you."

"We're waiting," called Olivia.

Sofia whispered, "I love you, Gramma Lisa." She tugged on the lead rope, and her horse followed her into the barn.

Sundance snorted at the crowd of admirers waiting outside his stall. Mom, Grace, and Pastor Amy held up their phones, capturing the moment in pictures. Grampy beamed, his bushy mustache unable to hide his wide smile. Olivia wiggled on her crutches, trying to get a better view. Ryan clutched a package wrapped in brightly colored, pony-themed paper.

Stephanie waved her arms. "Stand back and give the horse some room, for goodness sake."

Sofia led Sundance into the stall, shut the door, and removed his halter and lead rope. He circled, sniffing and snorting.

Ryan reached over the door. "I made this for Sundance."

Sofia ripped the wrapping paper to reveal a wooden sign. Sundance's name had been painted in rainbow colors over a picture of a palomino horse. Underneath were the words *owned by Sofia Ruiz*.

***

Sofia leaned against her horse's shoulder, the barn quiet except for the sound of Sundance contentedly chewing his hay. Pastor Amy had taken Olivia and Ryan to the mall for back-to-school shopping. Grace had left for work. Stephanie and Grampy were outside, making final arrangements with Gramma Lisa.

Mom peered over the stall door. "Could I pat him?"

"Of course," Sofia said. "Do you want to come into the stall with us?"

Mom inhaled sharply. "Is it safe? I mean, he's not going to bite me or anything?"

Sofia held back a giggle. "He's gentle. I promise."

Mom took a deep breath and stepped into the stall. "He's so big."

"Sundance, say hello to Mom."

Mom extended her fist toward Sundance's nose. He reached out and sniffed it.

Mom snatched it back.

"Like this." Sofia reached for Mom's hand. "Open your palm and keep your fingers flat."

"His nose is so soft." Sundance began to lick Mom's palm. "Oh, that tickles."

Sofia laughed. "He's looking for a treat."

"Honey Bear, do you think I could ride him sometime? I've never ridden a horse before."

Really? Mom had never ridden with Gramma Lisa? Maybe Mom ran away from home before Gramma Lisa owned horses. What other things did Sofia not know about Mom and her childhood?

Sofia scratched behind Sundance's ear. "I can teach you."

"I'd like that." Mom began to stroke his neck.

Gramma Lisa cleared her throat from outside the stall. "I just wanted to say goodbye to Sofia and Sundance."

So soon? Sofia bit her lip. Sundance was back in her life, but what about Gramma Lisa?

Mom glanced at Sofia before stepping away from Sundance. She stood with her hand hovering over the stall door, as if frozen in place. "He's a beautiful horse. Thank you for giving him to Sofia."

Gramma Lisa nodded and looked away. "I'm so sorry, Mandi. Sorry for everything."

Mom opened the door and closed it behind her. Her lip quivered.

"You were right." Gramma Lisa rubbed her eyes. "I can't believe what a fool I was. I ended things as soon as I knew the truth about who Mike was. But if it hadn't been for you, I don't know what might have..."

Gramma Lisa covered her face with her trembling hands and sobbed.

Sofia jumped, startling Sundance as she rushed out of the stall. She threw her arms around Gramma Lisa. "I'm okay. He didn't hurt me."

A moment later, Mom joined in Sofia's embrace. Gramma Lisa's shuddering breaths eased as Sofia clung to her. *Forgive each other. Please.*

"Look at this." Grampy stood in front of the door. "Any chance I can join the group hug?"

"Grampy!" Sofia ran to the barn entrance and grabbed his hand, dragging him forward to form a tight circle with Mom and Gramma Lisa.

Sundance whinnied.

"I think he wants to join us," Sofia said.

Gramma Lisa sniffed. "I sure am going to miss that guy."

"But you'll visit him soon, won't you?" Sofia asked. "And us?"

Mom nodded to Gramma Lisa and squeezed Sofia's hand. "I'm sure she will."

"You're welcome anytime," Grampy added.

Gramma Lisa's eyes glistened with fresh tears. "I hope you can visit me sometimes, too."

Mom released Sofia's hand. "Are any of you getting hungry? I was thinking that we could all go out for dinner."

Sofia laughed. "I know a great seafood place. They have dancing lobsters and the best fried clams in the world."

Glossary of horse terms

Here are some of the horse terms used in this book.

Gender:

gelding- a castrated (neutered) male horse

mare- an adult female horse

Horse breeds:

Appaloosa- a breed of horse with a spotted coat pattern. This term can also describe the color of a spotted miniature horse.

miniature horse- a tiny horse that stands less than 38 inches tall when measured from the last hair on the horse's withers. Some miniature horse breed registries require the horse to be 34 inches or smaller.

mini- a common term for a miniature horse

Morgan- an American breed of horse, especially common in New England

Quarter Horse- a popular American breed of horse, originally bred for ranch work and racing over short distances

Horse colors:

bay- a brown horse with black on the lower legs, and a black mane and tail

buckskin- a yellow, golden, or tan horse with black on the lower legs, with black mane and tail

chestnut- a reddish or brown colored horse

palomino- a yellow, golden, or light tan colored horse with white mane and tail

pinto- a horse with patches of white and one or two other colors

sorrel- a reddish, chestnut colored horse, often with a lighter colored mane and tail

Around the barn:

halter- a headstall used for leading and tying a horse, usually made of rope, nylon, or leather *harness-* a set of straps a by which a horse is fastened to a cart or wagon

lead rope- a rope or long strap that clips to the halter, used to lead or tie a horse

muck- to remove manure and soiled material from a horse's stall or pasture

paddock- an enclosure where horses are kept or exercised.

pasture- a large, enclosed area where horses can graze.

<u>Where to find a horse's digital pulse:</u>

In chapter 14, Sofia struggles to remember how to check Snickers' digital pulse. This drawing shows the points where it can be most easily felt. If the horse is healthy, it is difficult to feel a digital pulse. A horse with laminitis often has a strong, or "bounding" digital pulse.

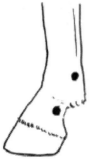

Acknowledgements

It can seem like the words of our favorite books flow effortlessly from the author's imagination directly onto the pages. In truth, most stories have gone through a lengthy process involving multiple drafts, revisions, and line-by-line editing. *A Place for Sofia* is my debut novel. I'm tremendously thankful for the many people who helped me to improve my writing and shape Sofia's story along the way.

I want to acknowledge the many online critique partners at Critique Circle who offered invaluable suggestions, insights, and constructive criticism, guiding me through two drafts of this novel. I particularly want to thank Ellie Summers for her constant encouragement and editing expertise, Chuck Robertson for asking insightful questions and teaching me how to hyphenate adjectives, Laurel Wanrow for connecting me to many resources and sharing her experiences as an independent author, and F.J. Reid for setting me straight about the ins and outs of admission to elite English boarding schools.

Because I wrote this book for kids who love horses, I sought the assistance of young beta readers. A "horsey" friend of mine, Michelle Denson, offered the manuscript to some of the students in her seventh-grade language arts classroom. These insightful girls not only provided their general reactions and opinions, but also editing suggestions, corrections of typos, and detailed feedback about the characters and plot. Thank you so much Adrianna Capozzi, Lou Lou Geannaris, Jade Moy, Audrey Rice, and Amanda Wang. Two sixth graders also gave their valuable insights as beta readers. Thank you to Megan Bruns and Sophia DeFillippo.

I want to thank my talented niece, Jordan Wilson, for assistance with the book cover design concept, and my sister, Mary Holt-Wilson, for her valuable observations and suggestions about the opening chapters of the novel. Thanks to Chrystal Lee for her advice about everything from logos to websites, and especially for her numerous pep-talks. *Yes! I can do this!*

Thank you to my husband, John, who endured countless hours of obsessive, mostly one-sided conversations about the process of writing and independent publishing and discussions about Sofia and her world. No relief is in sight, as I have already begun writing a sequel.

Most of all, I want to thank my daughter, Alanna, and her minia-ture horse, Max. Max came into our lives when Alanna was three years old. Eighteen years later, they're still partners. I wrote this story with a younger Alanna in mind. What kind of book would she have loved to read as an eleven year old? As Alanna and I shoveled manure, raked hay, groomed Max, and took him on walks together, we discussed Sofia, Olivia, Snickers, Kit Kat, and the other characters. What motivated them? How would Sofia's story end? Alanna read every draft of each chapter of the book, offering her reactions and responses to the story as I developed it. Max read none of it, but he still gets a great big thank you for the way he inspires me every day.

Dear Reader

Did you enjoy this book? Please recommend it to a friend and consider leaving a review through your favorite book retailer.

Are you curious to learn more about caring for miniature horses and horses in general? Do you love all things equine, and want to share your passion with others through your photography, artwork, poems, and stories? Do you want to brag (just a bit!) about your horse or the horse you wish was yours? I invite you to check out my website www.riverponykids.com[1].

The mission of River Pony Kids is to educate, encourage, and inspire horse lovers of all ages and abilities. River Pony Kids is a safe and accepting online space where readers can share their horse stories, accomplishments, and creative expressions with fellow horse lovers. Get inspired by others who are following their horse-related passions. Test your horse knowledge. Follow the lives of our "spokesponies", Max and Dusty. Ask questions about my writing, and learn more about my upcoming books.

I hope to "meet" you at riverponykids.com!

---

1.   http://www.riverponykids.com

About the Author

Lifelong horse enthusiast Laura Holt-Haslam is passionate about sharing her love of horses through art, writing, and hands-on learning. Her middle grade novel, *A Place for Sofia*, explores the transformative power of horses and friendship. Laura lives in Southern Maine with her husband, young adult daughter and son, two adorably naughty kittens, and the friendliest dog you'll ever meet. She and her daughter share ownership of Max, a 24 year old palomino miniature horse who loves to jump. You can read more at riverponykids.com.

Made in the USA
Lexington, KY
23 November 2019